Sarmiento

F   Poynter, Margaret.
Poy   A time too swift

PERMA-BOUND®

DATE DUE			
JAN 24 '94			
SEP 26 '98	-		
MAR 24 2003			

A Time Too Swift

Books by Margaret Poynter

Gold Rush!

Search & Rescue

Voyager
(with Arthur L. Lane)

Too Few Happy Endings

Wildland Fire Fighting

Under the High Seas
(with Donald Collins)

Cosmic Quest
(with Michael J. Klein)

What's One More?

A Time Too Swift

Margaret Poynter

Atheneum   1990   *New York*

Atheneum
Macmillan Publishing Company
866 Third Avenue, New York, NY 10022
Collier Macmillan Canada, Inc.
First Edition
Printed in the United States of America
Designed by Kimberly M. Hauck
10 9 8 7 6 5 4 3 2 1

Library of Congress Cataloging-in-Publication Data
Poynter, Margaret.
A time too swift/Margaret Poynter.

p.   cm.

*Summary: Living in San Diego on the verge of World War II, fifteen-
year-old Marjorie is confused by her romantic feelings for a
handsome serviceman and the changing attitudes toward the Japanese
neighbors she has known all her life.*

ISBN 0-689-31146-X

*{1. World War, 1939–1945—United States—Fiction.   2. Japanese
Americans—Fiction.}   I. Title.*
PZ7.P885Ti   1990
{Fic}—dc19   89–30896   CIP   AC

To Betty and Marjorie,
who share these memories with me
And to Ellen,
who shared my dreams

A Time Too Swift

Chapter 1

*P*ATIENCE IS A VIRTUE—THAT'S WHAT MY MOTHER HAS TOLD me over and over for as long as I can remember. But whenever there's something I want with all my heart, I find it next to impossible to wait for it calmly and passively.

This particular day was a perfect example of what I mean. There I was sitting on the bus bench at Horton Plaza feeling twitchy and wanting to jump up every time I heard the dinging of a streetcar bell. Ellen *has* to be on that one, I said to myself. If she isn't . . . well, I'll just have to go to the roller-skating rink without her.

Usually, waiting in the plaza doesn't do this to me. The splashing of the water in the big fountain behind me, the buttery aroma coming from the old-fashioned popcorn wagon on the corner, the pigeons cooing and bobbing their heads as they search for crumbs in the grass—there's no shortage of things to keep my senses busy. But this Saturday was different from all the other Saturdays I'd sat here on this wooden bench, because Prentice had said he'd be at the Skating Palace again this afternoon.

Prentice. The smell of the witch hazel he patted on his face. The rough texture of his uniform jacket. The way our hands fit together as we circled the rink. My heart slowed down then speeded up at the mere thought of the marine I'd met just last week. At first he hadn't seemed much different from all the other servicemen who crowded the Skating Palace, except that he didn't talk as much as most of them. I was the one who had to start the conversation, then keep it going.

"Where are you from?" I had asked.

"Hibbing, Minnesota."

"How do you like San Diego?"

"Fine."

He didn't volunteer any more information, so I'd asked him if he had a favorite band.

"Benny Goodman—he plays a fine clarinet."

I would have asked him how long he'd been in the Marine Corps, but the answer to that one was obvious—his boot camp haircut hadn't even started to grow out yet.

Since I was running out of questions, I was relieved when the organist announced that he was taking a break. As we moved toward the side of the rink, I expected Prentice to say thank you and that would be the end of our brief encounter. Instead, he asked me if he could buy me a Coke, and to be polite, I said yes. It wasn't until after I'd had a few sips from the bottle that I noticed his smile—the way it started out slow, then got wider and wider until it was reflected in his bluish gray eyes. I could tell that when Prentice smiled he meant it, and I began to realize that there really was no need for a river of words passing between us just to fill up the silence.

Another Fifth Avenue streetcar clanged to a stop, and, thank goodness, there was Ellen, wearing the yellow V-neck sweater that complemented her thick reddish hair. As she stepped onto the passenger island in the middle of Broadway, I glanced at my watch. In just a couple of minutes, the rink would open. I'd told Prentice that I was always on time. When he didn't see me, would he leave? My stomach ached at the thought.

"You're late!" I called to Ellen, motioning for her to hurry. A couple of sailors standing near the information booth grinned at me. Even as I felt myself blush, I knew that the best thing about the plaza was that it was always crowded with servicemen. A man in navy blue or marine olive green seems to stand so much taller —look so much more heroic—than a boy in corduroys and a button-down shirt.

"Sorry you had to wait," Ellen said. "We got our allotment check this morning so Mom took me to get some new shoes."

Even though I knew that for at least two weeks Ellen had had to put cardboard in the soles of her old shoes to patch up the holes, I couldn't get excited about her new ones. Right now, the important thing was that Prentice might be standing in front of the rink, looking up and down the street, wondering if I was going to show up.

"They look great," I said. "But let's get a move on."

Falling into step, Ellen and I walked down Third Avenue and across D Street, passing a string of junky gift shops, penny arcades, and cheap photography studios. As usual, they were full of servicemen, and a lot of them gave us the once-over. One of them even whistled and said, "Hubba, hubba." My mother had told me to ignore such "unwanted attentions," but it was hard to keep my eyes focused straight ahead when those attentions made me feel as tantalizing as Betty Grable or as alluring as Rita Hayworth.

Just as I was about to tell Ellen to walk faster, she broke the awful news.

"Dad's about to get some new orders," she said.

She spoke slowly and quietly, as she usually did, so at first the importance of what she had said didn't sink in. But then a little warning signal sounded way back in my head.

"That means I might be leaving San Diego."

Ellen's expression didn't change—she always kept her emotions locked up inside of her, so it was hard to know what she was thinking. What I did know was that the news jolted me so much that it dulled the sharpness of my anxiety about Prentice. After all, Ellen had been my best friend for over a year, ever since I'd seen her sitting by herself in our school's lunch pergola and I'd said hi and she'd said hi back.

In contrast to her quiet acceptance of conditions, I believe in letting my feelings spill out. "But you can't leave! You just can't. Why doesn't your dad have a regular job so you can stay here all the time?" Of course, I already knew the answer to that question. While my dad was wearing overalls and supervising the night cleanup crew in an office building, Ellen's father was wearing his chief petty officer's uniform and might be part of a North Atlantic convoy, fighting off German submarines, helping to get supplies to the British. It isn't that I don't love my father, but there's that thing I have about uniforms and the men who wear them.

"When he retires, he and Mom will settle down someplace. I guess by then I'll be all grown up."

"But what about *now?* Aren't you going to miss going to the zoo and the ferry rides and all the other stuff we do?"

"Well, sure, but what choice do I have?"

I didn't have an answer to that. As we turned onto G Street, I turned my attention back to a more immediate concern. Since the rink had been open for almost ten minutes, there was no one waiting in line to get in. Three sailors were standing a half-block away, and a woman was pushing a baby buggy across the intersection. There was no sign of Prentice. Maybe he's inside, I thought, as I handed two quarters to the man in the small box office. Oh, please, he *has* to be inside, or my whole day—my whole weekend—will be ruined. By now, Ellen's news had faded into the back of my consciousness. It could be dealt with in the future. This was *now*, and the not-knowing was almost too much to bear.

I followed Ellen into the rink, glancing at each marine, not noticing whether or not they glanced back, not caring that they might think I was being bold. Even when I bumped into a sailor, all I did was mumble "Sorry" as I looked past him for a certain cocking of the head, a certain hesitant smile.

It was habit that led me to the skate rental counter, habit that caused me to sit beside Ellen as we laced up our skates. I was aware only of Prentice's absence and the fact that the organist was playing "The Last Time I Saw Paris," one of the songs he'd played last week.

"My father thinks that song is nothing but propaganda," I had told Prentice. "He says it's supposed to make us want to get into the war against Germany. I think he's wrong . . . countries like France and England wouldn't use propaganda, would they?"

Prentice hadn't answered right away—that's one of the things I liked about him—he really seemed to listen, and when he said something, you could tell he'd thought it through and he meant what he said.

I finished lacing my skates and looked toward the door, hopeful and fearful at the same time. Still no sign of Prentice.

"I guess the thing I'll miss most about San Diego is going skating with you." When Ellen stood up and spun around, her skirt flared out, showing off her legs. I wished Dad would let me wear a skirt instead of slacks when I went skating. Maybe if Prentice had seen me in my pleated Scotch-plaid skirt instead of my baggy blue slacks, he would be here right now.

"Yeah . . . jeepers, I just thought, I bet Mom won't let me come down here by myself." Right away, I felt a little guilty for thinking about myself when it was Ellen who was going to have to go to another strange school and get used to another strange town.

"Maybe you could talk Dave into taking you," Ellen said.

How like Ellen, trying to figure out a way to make things better for me. I felt even more guilty.

"Even if he would—and he won't because he always goes places with Larry on the weekends—I won't have any fun at all without you." Unless Prentice were here, I thought. More guilt was piled onto the other layers.

We headed toward the opening in the worn wooden railing that surrounded the skating area. I took one more look at the entrance. "He's not there," I said, forcing the words around the lump in my throat.

"Who? Oh, Prentice. But it's early. He could have missed a bus." Her casual tone told me she had no idea that I was being devastated by disappointment . . . no, nothing as ordinary as disappointment. I was in a state of despair.

Almost as soon as we entered the skating area, a sailor came up from behind Ellen and took her hand. It was Jack, the same sailor she'd been skating with for the last three Saturdays. From the way her eyes shone when he was around, I knew she liked him a lot, although she hadn't come right out and said so. With the slightest of backward glances, my best friend left me alone with my misery.

So now there I was, skating alone. To make matters worse, who should show up but Beverly Rhodes. Beverly Rhodes, who glided through life while I stumbled; who sparkled while I faded into the background; whose blond curls never lost their bounce while my brunette ones went limp at the first hint of dampness in the air. It didn't help that she was allowed to wear lipstick while I couldn't use it for six more months.

Despite the fact that Beverly was there and Prentice wasn't, I kept circling the rink, deliberately arranging my expression to hide my inner turmoil. When the organist told everyone to clear the floor for a couples-only skate, I sat on the nearest bench, pushed the sleeves of my cardigan up on my arms, fluffed up my hair, and acted aloof, which wasn't easy with my head full of images of Prentice's eyes crinkling up as he smiled and the way he had held out his hand and cocked his head when he had first asked me to skate. By this time last Saturday, we'd been waltzing around the rink, swooping, swirling, dipping. . . .

The spotlight followed us as we went into the final minutes of our routine. Despite the importance of winning this competition, I had almost forgotten the thousands of people out there in the audience, the panel of judges who were watching our every move. All that seemed unimportant compared to the feeling of being one with this man, of the certainty that fate had brought us together.

The music rose to a crescendo and . . .

"Want to skate?"

It was the sailor I'd bumped into earlier. "Sorry," I said. "I'm waiting for someone."

"Oh. Well, thanks anyway." He stood by the railing as the organist started to play "In the Mood."

The song was almost over before the bouncy beat of the melody got to me. After all, I reasoned, I had paid for three hours of skating. Why waste all that good music? The sailor was still standing there, and the next time he turned to look at me, I smiled. Inclining his head toward the circling skaters, he smiled back, and I nodded. A minute later he was telling me his name was Frank and that he was from Omaha and that he had been in San Diego for almost a month.

"I never imagined a place could be so crowded," he said. "Why, there's almost as many people out at midnight as there are at noon."

I was just about to tell him it hadn't always been that way, when I saw Prentice standing outside the railing and the words stuck in my throat. Here it was, the moment I'd been waiting for all week, and I'd been so impatient that I was skating with this sailor who was nice enough, but he didn't wear witch hazel and he was talking so much that I couldn't get a word in edgewise.

But the worst thing was that Prentice didn't seem to know that I was even in the rink—he was staring straight at Beverly Rhodes, who was waltzing with a marine corporal. Why did that bother me so much? Why was it suddenly so hard to take a deep breath? After all, Prentice Moreland certainly wasn't the only good-looking, sweet-smiling serviceman in town.

I looked up at Frank. "Tell me more about Omaha," I said. "It sounds like a terrific place."

Chapter 2

I TRIED HARD TO CONCENTRATE ON WHAT FRANK WAS SAYING, but every time we passed the front of the rink, most of my attention shifted to Prentice. He was leaning on the railing, twirling his barracks cap around his finger. If he saw me at all, he gave no sign of recognition.

Since I wasn't really thinking about skating, what happened next was probably my fault. Somehow my skate clipped Frank's skate, and down I went, right on my rear end. Frank pulled me up, and Beverly was suddenly there, fake sympathy showing in her eyes. When Ellen took my arm and guided me toward the railing, I shrank up inside myself, acutely aware that everyone in the rink, including Prentice, had witnessed my clumsiness. As an attention-getter, nothing beats falling down.

"You're all dusty," Ellen said, brushing the back of my slacks with her hand.

"It's okay," I said, backing away from her, bumping into a little boy who darted behind me from out of nowhere. Oh, why couldn't I have been knocked unconscious when I fell? Then, at least, I would have been an object of pity instead of humiliation.

But then Prentice was standing beside me, concern darkening his expression. "You all right?" he asked. "Come on, let's sit down."

"No, no, I'm fine," I said, hoping that the slight chill in my voice would make him realize if he'd been on time, none of this would have happened.

"Sorry I'm late. There was some sort of foul-up with the passes." It was almost as if he could read my mind.

"Want to skate?" Prentice held out his hand, just as he had the first time I saw him.

I nodded, my fingers reaching for his, all of my embarrassment, my irritation, magically erased.

I'd figured that Prentice was a much better skater than he was a talker, but as the afternoon advanced, his tongue loosened up. He told me about the winter blizzards in his home state and how he wanted to go to college when his four-year hitch was over and that his favorite song was "Moonlight."

I told him that I wanted to be an English teacher and write short stories during summer vacations, and when I mentioned my brother, Dave, he told me about his sister. "Susan's a couple of years younger than me," he said. "About your age, I guess. In some ways, you remind me of her."

Great, I thought. Does he think of me as a sister? When I hold Prentice's hand, Dave's the last person on my mind.

Two hours with Prentice passed by quicker than ten minutes ever had with anyone else. Before I knew it, the organist was playing "Good Night, Sweetheart," signaling closing time. During the song's final chords, Prentice seemed to pull back into himself, rationing his words, hoarding his thoughts. I felt like Cinderella must have when the clock was about to strike midnight—full of longing for what might have been if only she'd been allotted a little more time. Just one more hour.

As the song ended, Prentice's arm tightened around my waist. Maybe, I thought, maybe he'll walk me to my bus. That would give us at least twenty more minutes before we have to say goodbye. Before I have to face another long week of waiting.

He guided me to the bench, then kneeled to unlace my skates. Again, I thought of Cinderella and how her prince had knelt before her as he slid the glass slipper onto her foot. Had her fingers longed to reach out and stroke the top of his head as mine did to touch the soft bristliness of Prentice's GI haircut?

He pulled my left skate off, revealing, to my horror, the small hole in the end of my sock. Praying that he hadn't noticed it, I curled my toes and tucked my foot under the bench, remembering how my mother was always warning me not to wear holey underwear or socks. "Think how you'd feel if you were in an accident and the doctor saw how careless you were," she'd say. Better a grandfatherly looking doctor than Prentice, I thought. Oh, why hadn't I listened to Mom's good advice?

Prentice had just finished turning in our skates at the rental counter when Ellen walked up to me. "Jack's asked me to go out for a hamburger." Her tone was matter-of-fact, but the slight flush in her cheeks told me much more than her simple statement.

"Hey, I'm starved." Prentice handed me my shoes. "Why don't we go, too?"

"I—I can't." I put on my shoes, my mind racing for something other than the real reason, but I couldn't come up with anything. "I promised my mom I'd come right home." Now he'll know, I thought. He'll know that even though I'm fifteen years old, my parents still treat me like a baby.

"Oh." A shadow crossed over Prentice's face. "Well, can I at least walk you to your bus stop?" Was that a trace of sarcasm in his voice?

I nodded and said sure, confused about the vague change that had come over him. It didn't help at all when Beverly Rhodes sauntered up to us, her short skirt swishing back and forth, making me feel frumpy in my dusty slacks.

"I'm sure glad you didn't hurt yourself when you fell," she said.

"Thanks." I moved toward Prentice, giving her notice that I had seen him first.

"See you around," Beverly called over her shoulder as she walked away. She was looking at me, but I was sure her words were aimed at Prentice.

Jack and Ellen stayed with us until we got to Broadway, then they stopped off at a hamburger shop. Prentice took my arm as we crossed a street, but let it go when we reached the curb on the other side. I had pictured us walking up the street, fingers entwined, a companionable silence enfolding us, shielding us from the outside world. But he didn't take my hand, and instead of the silence bringing us together, it stood between us like an impenetrable wall.

"The weather's nice, isn't it?" I said. That was a pretty dumb thing to say when the afternoon fog was rolling in and any minute now my hair would become as straight and stringy as a kitchen mop.

"Sure is," Prentice replied.

More silence. What's wrong? I wanted to cry out. Are we going to waste the little time we have left?

We stepped down from the curb to cross Second Avenue, and once again he took my arm, but I knew now it was just to be gentlemanly. But this time he let his hand slide down until it touched mine and he moved closer so the sleeve of his jacket was brushing against the sleeve of my sweater and my breath caught in my throat and . . .

"I don't suppose . . . well, would you mind giving me your telephone number? Maybe I could call you sometime."

Like a wave pulling back from the shore, all the sounds of the street receded. The babble of voices, the occasional toot of a car horn, the dinging of a streetcar bell all seemed far away, part of another world. The knowledge that he wanted my telephone number filled my head and left no room for anything else, except the knowledge that I couldn't give it to him. Dad would have a fit if he knew I was interested in a serviceman.

"Well, the thing is my father works nights and he doesn't like the telephone to ring unless it's an emergency, because it might wake him up and then he couldn't get back to sleep and—" The words tumbled out, each one stepping on the heels of another, each one seeming to increase the look of puzzlement on Prentice's face.

"I understand." Although he didn't change position, I could sense him backing away. "You don't have to explain anything to me. I had a real good time skating, but I can sure understand why you don't . . ."

My ears heard what he was saying, but my brain didn't register its meaning because I was too busy deciding whether or not to tell him the truth and wondering what he'd do if I was honest with him and praying that the bus wouldn't come until I got this whole situation straightened out. "Oh, heck, I might as well tell you . . . my father won't let me date for six more months, not until March when I turn sixteen, and if he found out I gave my number to someone I'd just met . . . well . . ."

I took a deep breath, relieved that I'd finally been honest with him, but convinced that I'd never see him again. As I waited for him to respond to my confession, I averted my eyes, unable to face what I knew I'd see in his expression—a distancing as he groped for a way to say his final good-bye. Then, when the "A" bus pulled from the side street onto Third Avenue, I forced myself to look at him and found instead that his face was alight with relief and understanding. "Wow," he said. "That makes me feel heaps better."

I stared at him. "What do you mean?"

"I thought you were giving me the old heave-ho."

A fat lady and her three small children brushed past me as my bus pulled up to the curb. They were followed by an old man with a shopping bag and a couple of women chattering to each other in Italian. Finally there was no one left but me. "I'd never do that," I said, putting one foot into the stairwell and talking fast because the bus driver was shifting gears and looking impatient. "We're the only Ellisons in the book. Hang up if anyone but me answers. And I'll be at the rink next Saturday."

The door closed behind me before Prentice could say anything else. I rushed to the back of the bus and caught a final glimpse of him standing on the curb looking after me. Prentice likes me. Prentice likes me! The thought made me slightly dizzy, and I plopped down in the nearest seat. If only I could go out with him. If only . . . if only . . .

The moonlight filtered through the branches of the palm trees as we strolled hand in hand through Balboa Park. For several minutes neither of us spoke, and I welcomed the silence because words might break the spell that had crept over us as softly as the evening fog had drifted up from the bay. Although we had known each other but a short time, I was already longing to feel his strong arms circling my waist, to have his lips touch mine, to . . .

I dared think no further. For now it was enough to sense that maybe . . . just maybe . . . Prentice might be having the same daydream that I was.

Chapter 3

I WAS COUNTING THE MINUTES AND THE HOURS AND THE DAYS I'd have to live through until next Saturday, when the bus driver called out "Pringle Hill," and as I trudged up the five blocks to Guy Street. It was a long walk, but Mom said the view was worth it, and I agreed with her. From the big picture window in our front room, we could see the city spread out to our left and watch the planes take off from Lindbergh Field. The silver-colored buildings of Consolidated Aircraft sprawled along the edge of the bay on one side, and on the other side, Point Loma jutted out into the Pacific Ocean.

When I got to our corner, I turned and looked to my right, where the marine base lay between Consolidated and the naval training station. Prentice was stationed at the base. Tomorrow he'd be eating in the mess hall, forcing down what he described as "powdered eggs and powdered milk and something lumpy and brownish that was supposed to be stew."

"Boy, do I ever miss Mom's pot roast," he had said with a dreamy look in his eyes.

I had a sudden need to hear his voice again. How was I going to live through the next six days?

I turned around, inhaled the sweet aroma of the honeysuckle

bushes that lined one side of the battleship-gray duplex on the corner, then arrived at our brown-shingled bungalow and stepped onto the porch. When I opened the front door, Dave was sprawled on the couch reading a Superman comic book, his feet propped up on the threadbare armrest. "Hi, kid," he said.

"Don't call me 'kid.' " I had told him that at least a million times with no results.

Dave grinned and turned a page. Mom's voice floated in from the kitchen. "That you, Marjorie? How about setting the table?"

I had been setting the table ever since I was five years old, so you'd think Mom would know better than to remind me every single night. But maybe her telling me was like my telling Dave not to call me kid. No one paid any attention to those little exchanges; they were just a way to communicate, to let each other know that our lives were on the usual track.

Of course, at the moment, my life seemed to be taking a detour into uncharted territory. Carefully, deliberately, keeping my delicious secret hidden deep inside of me, I took the chipped everyday plates from the cupboard and placed them around the table. "Is Dad asleep?" I asked, not because I wanted to know, but because I had to carry out my pretense that this was just another day in an unending succession of ordinary days.

"Nope. He's next door fixing a leaky faucet for Mrs. Wilson. Hey, guess what. Larry talked his folks into signing for him. Now all he has to do is pass the physical and he'll be off to boot camp."

There was a faint click in my mind, a shadowy sense of change that had nothing to do with Prentice. I shrugged the feeling off. After all, Larry was Dave's friend, not mine. His leaving would make little difference in my life, just as Ellen's leaving would make little difference in Dave's. I placed a setting of silverware beside each plate. "It's hard to imagine Larry in the navy. I mean, he's lived up the street for as long as I can remember, and now he won't be there anymore."

Dave got up and paced across the sun-faded carpet, cracking his knuckles the way he always did when he was upset about something. "Why can't Dad see things my way for once? If he'd sign for me, Larry and I might be able to go through training together—even get assigned to the same ship. Boy, could we ever have some good times in all those foreign ports."

"That's enough of that kind of talk!" Dad must have come in the back way, and, as usual, his presence filled the room, making me feel small and insignificant. "Your job is to finish school. Do you want to be like me—little better than a broom pusher?"

"But Dad," Dave said, "I can always finish school after my hitch is over. A lot of guys in the senior class are enlisting."

"That's their business." Dad pulled his chair out and sat down at the table. "I'm not taking a chance that my son will be sent to fight someone else's battle." Whipping his napkin open, he tucked it beneath his chin, his square-set jaw proclaiming that the discussion was over. Case closed.

No one said another word until Mom came in a couple of minutes later. After placing a steaming bowl of chicken and dumplings near Dad's right hand, she pushed her short brown hair away from her face with a fluttery gesture. "There now," she said. "Let's all enjoy each other's company." The comment was her plea for peace in the family. Sometimes I thought she didn't care who was right or who was wrong, as long as there was no arguing.

I picked up the milk pitcher and filled my glass. Dave's lucky though, I thought. At least he'll be eighteen in February and then he won't need anyone's permission to join up, and I still won't even be old enough to go out with Prentice if he's still stationed here and if he still wants to take me out.

Dad turned on the oval-shaped Philco that stood near the head of the table. Mom pressed her lips together. She was always saying that the only time we got together anymore was at mealtime, and she wanted us to have a "little polite conversation," as she put it. What Mom wanted didn't make any difference though. Dad was the boss, and when he wanted to listen to the radio, that's exactly what he did.

"So, don't forget," said the announcer, "when you're shopping for a tooth cleanser, reach for Teel, the exciting, the new, the unique liquid dentifrice. And now for a commentary."

"Good evening, this is Gordon Green. The isolationists in our country embrace many diverse personalities. Some want to avoid war at any cost. Others consider the German war machine to be invincible. Members of the German-American Bund do not want the power of the United States used to defeat the Axis. Still others seem to feel that if we ignore the world situation, it will simply go away.

"Despite the exhortations of these groups to stay out of the struggle in Europe, arguments about American neutrality have become largely academic. We are arming Great Britain under the Lend-Lease program; our destroyers are convoying British ships halfway across the Atlantic; and British pilots are training in the United States. In the Pacific, economic sanctions are being taken against Japan. We are a nation at peace, prepared to go to war at any time. Since the drawing up of the Atlantic Charter last summer . . ."

"We should never have gotten involved in that charter business," Dad muttered, spearing a piece of chicken with his fork. "We have enough to keep us busy right here at home."

"You're so right, John," Mom said. "Why, just the other day

I was talking to Lenora next door and she said with all the problems this country has, what in the world are we doing getting mixed up with—"

"Just a minute." Dad turned up the volume a little. Mom didn't say anything else as the commentator finished up, and she was still quiet while the announcer talked about how good Domino cigarettes were and when the local newscaster came on the air.

"A slight earthquake jolted northern Baja California about four o'clock this morning. Residents of San Ysidro felt the tremors, but no damage has been reported."

"My science teacher says he wouldn't be surprised if southern California had a really big earthquake one of these days," Dave said.

Dad nodded. "He could be right. That one in Long Beach a few years ago was bad enough, but nothing compared to what it could have been."

The tension around the table dissolved, because earthquakes were something everyone could agree on. "Maybe you children don't remember, but we felt that one way down here," Mom said. "Some people had their windows broken."

"I remember," I said. "The dishes were bouncing around on the shelves, and I thought to myself, 'Something's wrong. Houses aren't supposed to wiggle.' "

As Dad tilted his head back and laughed, Mom glanced at me, her warm smile melting the tense lines in her face.

I lay there in the smoking rubble of my high school, too clearly aware that the Old Gray Castle had been leveled. As the aftershocks continued, I pulled myself up, gritting my teeth against the stabbing pain in my badly lacerated leg. Hobbling about, I sought out victims who were worse

*off than I. It was while I was comforting a slightly injured but very
hysterical Beverly Rhodes that a young naval medical officer asked me my
name.*

*"Why do you want to know?" I asked, remembering Dad's warnings
about talking to strangers.*

*"Because you deserve a commendation for your bravery," he replied,
stooping to apply a tourniquet to a victim's arm.*

*"I'm Marjorie Ellison," I said, "but I'd prefer not to get recognition
for what I'm doing."*

*The doctor looked at me, admiration filling his eyes. "Please, I must
see you again. Can we meet when this emergency is over?"*

I lowered my eyes in response to the intensity of his gaze. He . . .

"Majorie, didn't you hear me?" Dad sounded annoyed. "For the
second time, please pass the biscuits."

"I'm sorry," I said, handing him the plate. "I was thinking
about something." If I had told him what that something was,
he'd have given me a lecture on the evils of daydreaming. But how
could I turn off my imagination? With it, I could be anything I
wanted to be, do anything I wanted to do. I could even be so
beautiful, have such a vivacious personality, be such a terrific skater
that Prentice would wait as long as necessary to take me out.

"I don't care if you can't go out on dates with me," he'd say.
"I'll keep on adoring you until you can, and then we'll go to dinner
and we'll dance and walk along the beach in the moonlight, and
we'll . . ."

Well, knowing Prentice, he probably wouldn't say it in just
those words, but however it came out, it would sound more beautiful than a poem written by Longfellow or Keats.

The telephone rang, and I jumped up to answer it. "Probably
Ellen," I said.

"Marjorie?" It was a boy's voice. Could it be Prentice? Oh, it had to be Prentice. But what if it was and Mom and Dad caught on?

"Yes." I glanced toward the table. Dad was taking a sip of coffee and Mom was saying something to him. Dave never paid any attention to what I did or said. So far, so good.

"I took a chance that you'd answer. Can you talk?"

"No." My palms were slick with sweat. My heart pounded.

"Well, I wasn't doing anything, so I thought—I just wanted to let you know what a great time I had this afternoon."

If only I could tell him how deliriously happy I was that he had called. "Me, too" was all I dared to say.

"See you Saturday?"

"Yes. So long for now." I put the receiver back on the hook and walked back to the table.

"Well, that was quick," Dave said.

"Who was it, dear?" Was it my guilty conscience that made me think her eyes narrowed as she looked at me?

"Just someone . . . a girl from history class with a question about the . . . about our homework."

A few minutes ago I would have given anything to get that telephone call. Now I was having to lie and I knew my mother wasn't falling for it, but what could I do? I had to keep on seeing Prentice. . . . Slow down, I told myself. Act normal.

"Would you please clear away the plates, Marjorie?" Mom said.

That was something else she said every single night, and to me it was a signal that Mom didn't suspect anything. And even if she did, she wasn't going to make an issue of it right now, not at the dinner table.

Chapter 4

THE DANCE FLOOR WAS CROWDED, BUT WHEN I CLOSED MY eyes, it was as if Prentice and I were the only couple there. As he led me through the intricate steps of a tango, the full skirt of my filmy gown swirled around my legs, adding to the illusion that I had been transported to the surface of a cloud.

"I've waited all my life for a girl like you to come along," Prentice murmured.

"Fate brought us together," I replied.

"I'm expecting to go on a secret mission," he said. "It may take weeks . . . even months. Will you—will you please wait for me?"

Yes, yes, I wanted to cry out, but my breath caught in my throat.

"Please answer, Marjorie . . . Marjorie . . ."

"Marjorie!" Mrs. Gilmore's sharp voice jerked me back into reality. "We're waiting."

"Wh-what?"

"For the second time, please recite Hamlet's soliloquy."

"Oh . . . 'To be or not to be, that is the question. Whether 'tis nobler to . . . to . . .' " As if someone had shut off a switch, my mind went blank. Someone in the back of the room tittered. I wanted to slide under my desk and disappear.

Mrs. Gilmore made a mark in her record book. "Very well, let's go on to someone else." There were at least ten hands waving in the air. Why had she chosen me when I hadn't volunteered? It wouldn't have been so bad if this had been the first time I'd had a memory lapse this week. On Monday I'd been trying to imagine how Prentice would look when his hair grew out and my algebra teacher had called on me to explain an equation he'd written on the blackboard. While everyone stared, I stammered out some answer that had nothing to do with what I'd been asked. And yesterday Miss Colbert had asked me to name the founders of the Plymouth Colony and all I could do was blurt out "Roger somebody, wasn't it?" because I'd been in the middle of wondering if it's really possible to fall in love at first sight, even though in the movies it happens all the time.

And now I'd disgraced myself in what's usually my best class. I was going to have to find a way to combine being in love with keeping my grades up.

The lunch bell finally rang and I gathered up my books, anxious to make a quick getaway. Just before I reached the door, though, Mrs. Gilmore's voice stopped me like a taut leash. "Marjorie, please step up to my desk for a moment."

"Yes, ma'am?" Feeling like a prisoner walking to the gallows, I approached her.

"Have you decided on the topic for your term project yet? You were supposed to tell me yesterday, you know."

"I promise I'll make up my mind this weekend."

"Very well. I'll expect your decision no later than Monday." A frown pulled her thick gray eyebrows together. "Your work has not been up to your usual high standards this week."

"I know, but I'll do better, I promise. Thank you." I turned away, clutching my notebook to my chest. More than anyone else,

Mrs. Gilmore had inspired me and given me the courage to express my feelings in writing. To restore her faith in my ability and to show my gratitude for her support, I was going to have to come up with a truly outstanding term project. And I was going to have to do that despite being in love.

After grabbing my lunch from my locker, I headed for the pergola. Making my way around clusters of kids, I found Ellen sitting in a far corner, eating her tuna-fish sandwich.

"Mrs. Gilmore kept me after class for a couple of minutes," I said, opening my sack. "I've got until Monday to come up with a topic for a term paper. The problem is I have only one good idea, and I think I need a partner to help me on it."

"Well, get one." Ellen believed that everything was simple: Whatever she wanted done was usually done—one, two, three, no complications, no nonsense. She couldn't understand why I always seemed to be clambering over obstacles. Actually, I couldn't either. That's just the way my life seemed to go.

"There is someone I'd like to ask—Kaye Narasaki. But she's such a brain. Do you think she'd really want to work with me?"

"Kaye?" Ellen stopped polishing her apple on the sleeve of her sweater. From the look in her eyes, I sensed she realized that this time maybe the obstacle wasn't an imaginary one. "You can't be serious."

I stared at Ellen. The sun filtering through the bougainvillea above us made leafy shadows on her face. The shadows slid back and forth with the breeze, but her eyes were motionless as she waited for my answer.

"What do you mean?" I couldn't let her know that I was hurt, almost insulted by her remark. Sure, I wasn't the smartest kid at San Diego High, but I'd always managed to keep up a B-minus average. Now here she was saying I wasn't good enough to work with Kaye.

"She's a Jap, that's what. Over in China, the Japs are torturing babies and burning people's houses."

For a moment I was too stunned to say anything, then I blurted out the first thing that came to my mind. "But—but the Narasakis don't have anything to do with that." The words sounded feeble compared to the torrent of arguments that were rushing through my head. The Narasakis are gentle people, hardworking people. They wouldn't kill a spider. Everyone likes them—well, obviously not everyone, but everyone who knows them.

Ellen wadded up a piece of waxed paper and tossed it into the trash can. Her jaw was set like Dad's when he gets stubborn. "They could be spies, you know."

"Not the Narasakis." I shook my head, for a moment unable to recognize her as my friend, then wanting to apologize for starting the discussion.

"You can believe what you want, but that doesn't make it true." Ellen's half-eaten apple went the way of the waxed paper, then she stood up. "I have to get to the library." Not waiting for me to answer, she walked away, her back stiff, her curls bouncing indignantly on her neck.

I started to call her back, to tell her I was sorry, that I didn't want to argue with her. But before I could get my apology out, she was too far away to hear it. I stared at the baked-bean sandwich Mom had fixed—last night's leftovers were always turning up in my lunch—and found it distasteful.

As I rewrapped my sandwich and put it back into my sack, I felt a quick surge of anger. Is it my responsibility to know what's going on in Ellen's mind? And even knowing how she feels, do I have to make a choice between her and the Narasakis, whom I'd known for most of my life? When Dave and I were just starting school, we'd made a little ceremony of spending our nickel-a-week allowance in their small store, which stood at the bottom of Pringle Hill. What a cornucopia of penny candy there was in the glass showcase—licorice ropes, saltwater taffy, chocolate kisses, buttery-tasting caramels, horehound. Oh, the tantalizing decisions we had to make as we clutched our pennies in our grimy hands.

If we had gone to the Ace Drug Store, an impatient clerk would have been tapping her foot and glaring at us as we struggled to make our choices. But not Mr. and Mrs. Narasaki—they always smiled their soft, slightly mysterious smiles and puttered around the produce section, telling us to take our time. They, more than any other adults, seemed to know how important these few minutes were to us.

One day I had paid for my purchases and Dave was still agonizing over whether to spend his whole allowance on a Honey Comb or to get an assortment of bubble gum. While I waited, I puzzled over the labels on the cans and packages of imported Oriental food that lined one corner of the store.

"Interesting, eh?" Mr. Narasaki said, tracing his index finger over the exotic-looking characters on a box of noodles. "This is the language of my people."

"What's this word?" I pointed to a symbol that looked like a scraggly bit of chaparral.

He had handed me a piece of butcher's paper and a pencil. "Here, you copy it and the next figure, and I'll tell you their meaning."

That was the first of a series of lessons in Japanese that lasted until I was twelve years old. From the labels on cans of mushrooms and packages of herbs, I went on to reading the headlines in

Japanese newspapers. RUSSIAN TROOPS GATHER ON SIBERIAN BORDER. MORE TAXES REQUIRED FOR ARMAMENTS. EMPEROR PRAISES IMPERIAL INFANTRY. As I had taken these peeks into the concerns of a people who lived on the other side of the Pacific Ocean, it occurred to me how hard it must be to be part of two different cultures. Did the Narasakis ever feel torn? I never asked the question.

And then one day when I was about twelve, Dad had told me to stop spending so much time with "that Japanese family"—he never once used their name. "Why?" I had asked, wondering what terrible thing I had done to deserve such a punishment.

His gaze slid away from me, and I knew it wasn't me who had been doing something wrong. "Because I told you so," he had said, but his words didn't have much force behind them, and I knew he didn't have a real reason. For a long while, I puzzled over strange adult standards, then, as I made new friends at Roosevelt Junior High, I stopped missing the old ones.

The warning bell rang and I grabbed my purse and notebook and hurried to my locker. When I opened it, a small avalanche of stuff tumbled out—books, papers, and a dirty gym blouse ended up on the floor. And then who should come around the corner but Beverly Rhodes with two Castle-ettes. "Something like Fibber McGee's closet, huh, Marjorie?" she said. "Need some help?"

"No, I'm okay," I mumbled, scooping an armful of books back into the locker.

Beverly and her friends went on down the hall, giggling at something Beverly had said. She's telling them about my accident at the skating rink, I thought. Why is it that the only time things like that happen is when she's around to witness them? She's probably convinced that I go through life stumbling, falling, spilling, and dropping.

I knew I might get into trouble with Dad and arouse Ellen's wrath, but at four o'clock that very afternoon, I got off the bus and walked toward the Narasakis' store. The neatly lettered sign in the window read JAPANESE-AMERICAN MARKET and in smaller letters, FRESH MILK, EGGS, VEGETABLES, AND MEAT. Below that were some Japanese characters that I remembered had the same meaning as the English words. A tidal wave of memories washed through me, and for a moment I wished I were back in the third grade, my mouth watering at the prospect of a sweet treat and my eyes eager for the sight of the Narasakis' welcoming smiles.

When I opened the screen door, the bell that was attached to it jingled and Kaye looked up from helping a Mexican lady pick out some potatoes. "Hi," she said, her eyebrows raised in surprise. "Be there in a couple of minutes."

As I waited near the counter, I realized it must have been almost four years since I'd set foot in this store. And now that I was here, it wasn't to buy anything or to pay a friendly visit—it was to get Kaye's help with an English-lit paper. I wouldn't blame her if she turned me down. After all, she got straight A's in all her classes. Why would she want to work with me?

A couple of minutes later, Kaye's parents came in from the back room. The delicate scent of the bouquet of sweet peas Mrs. Narasaki was carrying mingled with the light musky smell of the store. "Marjorie, how are you?" she said. "It's been a long time since we've seen you." She laid the flowers on the end of the counter.

"What a wonderful surprise." There was no accusation in Mr. Narasaki's expression, but I sensed he knew the reason for my long absence. "And you've become such a beautiful young lady; but of course, I predicted that long ago."

I felt the pressure of tears behind my eyes. In spite of my ignoring them all this time, they were making me feel like a long-lost friend. "Thank you," I said. "Is Paul around?"

"Oh, no. He's at Fort Ord. How we miss him," Mrs. Narasaki said.

"He's in the army? When did he get drafted?"

"He didn't wait for that. He enlisted." Mr. Narasaki shuffled toward the stairs that led to their upstairs living quarters. "I hope you'll excuse me, but I must take a short rest before the evening customers come in. We hope to see you again soon, dear friend." A bare bulb hung by a cord from the ceiling above him, its harsh light emphasizing the lines in his face.

Kaye put the customer's potatoes and bread into a paper sack and rang up the sale on the cash register. "Don't forget to come in tomorrow. We'll have some fresh yellowtail."

The woman grinned, showing a gap in her front teeth. "*Sí, gracias*. I be here."

Kaye turned to me. "Don't tell me—you just got your allowance and you're hungry for jelly beans."

I laughed, grateful for her lighthearted remark. "No, I was just wondering . . . well, what are you doing your English-lit paper on?"

"I was planning on comparing Shakespeare to some other writers of the same period."

"Have you started . . . I mean, I have this idea but it would be really hard to do by myself and Mrs. Gilmore said we could work with someone else."

Mrs. Narasaki smoothed down her apron as another customer came into the store. "Mrs. Olsen," she said. "I have some extra-sweet peaches today. They'd make such a good pie." The two women walked to the produce section on the other side of the room.

"What were you thinking about?" Kaye asked.

"I thought it would be great if we could be partners in writing an extra scene for *Hamlet*. It's something no one else would think of and it would be fun to do, but I'm sort of afraid to tackle it alone."

Kaye didn't say anything for a few seconds. When she spoke again, she looked away from me. "Why are you asking me? You have other friends."

"Because I know we could do a super-good job." I hesitated, then lowered my voice. "Besides, I've missed coming down here." Should I tell her that my father had told me to stay away? No, that might make things more uncomfortable than they already were.

"And my parents have missed your friendship, too," Kaye said. She looked at me, her dark eyes still wary. "All right, I'll tell Mrs. Gilmore I'm going to change my topic. When do you want to start?

"As soon as you have some time," I said, fishing in my purse for some change. "How about a quarter's worth of those chocolate creams?"

Kaye reached for a small paper bag. "You still like chocolate, I see. I guess some things don't change."

It was easy to figure what she meant by that. "A *lot* of things don't change," I said as I opened the door. "When you write to Paul tell him hello for me. Tell him I'd like to see him when he comes home on leave."

Smiling now, Kaye wrote something on a piece of paper. "Tell him yourself. Here's his address. I know he'd love to hear from you."

"Thanks." I stuck the paper in the front of my American history book. "See you in class tomorrow." As I opened the door, I glanced at Mrs. Narasaki.

"Come back soon and often," she said.

"I'll try. I really will." Even as I spoke those words, I remembered how upset Ellen had been when I'd told her I might work with Kaye. And Dad. What was he going to say? But this was for school. Didn't that make it all right?

Jeepers, why was I feeling so guilty and confused when I knew I wasn't doing anything wrong?

Chapter 5

*T*HAT EVENING I DID LITTLE TO CONTRIBUTE TO THE DINNER-table conversation, because my attention was on the telephone, which had been mute all afternoon. Ellen should be the one to call, I thought. After all, *she* was the one who had gone marching off to the library, leaving me to finish my lunch alone. But as the evening wore on, placing the blame for our disagreement grew less and less important. I had to know whether or not we were still friends. Ignoring my pride, just before my nine o'clock bed-time, I dialed Ellen's number.

"Hi . . . are you . . . ?

"Oh, I meant to call you," she said. "But there's been so much going on here. Dad's being shipped out to Pearl Harbor and Mom says we'll be going, too."

"No, you can't!" I cried. "I'll miss you!"

"I don't have any say about it." Ellen sighed. "I'll miss you too. And what about Jack—I might never see him again."

"Can't you talk your mom into staying here? Beg, plead, tell her anything, but get her to change her mind."

"Not a chance. She can't stand to be separated from Dad."

Ideas raced around inside my head. And there it was—the solution, flashing like a neon sign. "Hey, your mom could go, but you could stay here. At least for a while—maybe till the end of the semester." Say yes, say yes, I prayed, but there was no sound on the other end of the line.

When Ellen finally answered, her voice was subdued. "I . . . I don't know. Mom might not like it. She . . ."

What about Prentice? The words burst upon my consciousness, pushing whatever Ellen was saying into the background. Mom won't let me go to the Skating Palace by myself, so if Ellen leaves, I won't be able to see Prentice and my big romance will be over before it has a chance to start.

"Well, ask her . . . it won't hurt to ask, will it?"

"I guess not," Ellen said, but there was no conviction in her voice.

"Promise you'll . . ."

Mom came into the room from the kitchen, picked up a magazine from the coffee table, sat on the couch, and started flipping pages. How much had she heard?

"Ask her right away." How could I transmit the urgency I felt while keeping my voice normal for Mom's benefit? I said goodbye and placed the receiver on the hook.

"Something's wrong?" Mom asked.

I turned to face her. "No . . . well, yes. Ellen's dad got his orders."

Mom put the magazine on her lap. "Does that mean . . . ?

I nodded. "Ellen will probably leave, too."

"Oh, that would be awful . . . you two have been so close the last few months." Mom's expression was soft and concerned.

"I'll really miss her." I had to ask, had to know. "Mom, is there a chance . . . do you suppose . . . well, if Mrs. Hill says it's all right, could Ellen stay here for a while?"

Mom was quiet, but I knew that her mind was turning my

question over, looking at it from all sides. "Goodness," she said. "I don't know. It would be all right with me, but . . . well, the decision really lies with your father."

To Dad, there was only one side of an issue—his side. I could hear his objections now . . . "An extra mouth to feed . . . more noise . . . more work for your mother." Why was it always Dad who had the ultimate authority?

It was plain to me that, compared to what I had to face, Ellen's job would be a cinch. I had to pick the perfect time, catch Dad in the perfect mood, hope Mom would back me up . . . but it had to work out. It just *had* to.

It wasn't easy finding the right moment, but finally on Friday we were all sitting around the table after a roast-pork dinner— Dad's favorite—and everyone had just finished laughing over a joke that Dave had told. My intuition told me it was now or never. After a quick mental rehearsal of my lines, I took a deep breath and cleared my throat. "Dad?"

Dad put down his coffee cup. "Yes?"

"I have something important to ask you."

"Well, ask away."

Just get it over with. Blurt it out. The worst he can do is say no. "Ellen's dad's been shipped out. Her mom's getting ready to follow him, and I . . . well, Ellen wants to finish out the semester here. I was wondering . . . can she stay with us if her mom says it's all right?"

I waited. Dad added some more sugar to his coffee, stirred it, glanced at Mom, then back at me.

"Another giggly girl in the house? Two against one? No fair." Dave's kidding eased the tension, and for that I was grateful.

"The end of the semester. That's two-and-a-half months. A long time." Dad's voice was thoughtful, but not out-and-out negative.

"She'd help around the house," I said.

A faint smile touched Mom's lips. "I was thinking the very same thing."

My chest loosened up because I knew the battle was half won. Dad was the boss, but Mom had a way of talking him into things.

Dad wiped his mouth with his napkin and stood up. "Your mother and I will talk about it."

"When?" I forced the word out, afraid of upsetting him, but needing to know. "Mrs. Hill says she's going to get the tickets as soon as her allotment check comes, and that'll be next week."

Mom reached out and touched my hand. "Patience," she said softly.

Patience. That was easy for her to say. She had no way of knowing that my entire future might depend on Dad's answer. I wouldn't be able to sleep or to eat . . . I'd barely be able to breathe until I knew. Why, oh, why, was my fate always hanging on someone's else's whim, someone else's mood, someone else's order?

The next afternoon as Ellen skated with Jack, Prentice and I rexed and fox-trotted and tangoed and waltzed our way around the rink; the conversation flowed easily with no awkward gaps. This boy, who at first had seemed to have nothing to say, now appeared knowledgeable about many subjects, ranging from the status of the Brooklyn Dodgers to the possibility of the United States entering the war. And when I responded with my opinions, he listened, nodded his head, made me feel as if what I thought and said really mattered. The whole afternoon would have been perfect if only I knew that Ellen's mom would say yes, that Dad would say yes, that Ellen herself was one hundred percent in favor of my idea. If only—so many times those words had started my imagination rolling, had led to the creation of a full-fledged fantasy. Now they were boxing me in, making me realize how powerless and dependent I was.

And then the almost-perfect afternoon was over, and as Prentice and I were walking up Broadway toward the plaza, he again retreated into silence, replying to my remarks with noncommittal monosyllables, his mind obviously far away. Don't do this, I wanted to cry. Not when I won't see you for another week. Not when the only time I'll be able to talk to you is during a hurried, secretive telephone call.

It wasn't until three minutes before the bus was due that Prentice told me what was wrong. "I hate seeing a girl behind her folks' backs," he said, lowering his gaze. "Sneaking around—well, it just isn't right. I can't keep doing it."

Knowing Prentice as I now did, his statement didn't surprise me. I felt the same myself, and even if my conscience hadn't been so strong, Mom was too smart not to get suspicious about those telephone calls, those "wrong numbers" that everyone except me seemed to get. Now I felt as if Prentice was saying that I had to do something about his situation, or else. The gravity of his expression told me more than his words that he was giving me an ultimatum.

"But what can I do? If I tell them I've been meeting you, they won't let me go skating anymore."

"Isn't there any way I could come up to your house? Maybe if they got to know me. . ." He hesitated, appeared to waver in his resolution, then straightened his shoulders. "Well, that'll have to be up to you, won't it?"

If my folks got to know him . . . that was the answer all right, because they couldn't ask for a nicer boy than Prentice. But I couldn't just say I'd met a marine and he was coming to see me. Maybe Dad would say yes if it was a boy from school. But a serviceman? I'd heard his opinions about servicemen often enough. "They're away from home—accountable to no one. Here today and gone tomorrow, leaving innocent girls high and dry." His words always sounded vaguely threatening, but they certainly couldn't apply to Prentice. Sure, one of these days he'd be shipped out, but that certainly didn't mean he was untrustworthy.

"I'll talk to my mother." It was a feeble half-promise, but better than nothing.

"Good." He smiled and squeezed my hand, and somehow even though the plaza was as crowded as it ever was, we were alone in our own little world. But now the bus was coming, and I'd have to live through another week before I saw him again, and those seven days stretched before me as bleak as a desert landscape.

The bus pulled up to the curb, and Prentice and I stood back, buying a few more seconds as other passengers shoved toward the door. "See you Saturday," I said, aching to feel his arms around me.

"Right." He brushed his lips against my cheek and pushed me toward the bus. "Go on now, and don't forget about talking to your mom."

My cheek burned where he had kissed me, and instead of stepping into the stairwell, I floated into it. He had kissed me! This must be a dream!

But my dream quickly changed back into reality, because just as I took the last available seat, three more passengers got on, and one of them was Dave's friend, Larry. "Hi," he said, grasping the handle on the seat that was directly in front of me.

"Hi." Act ordinary, I told myself. Maybe he didn't see Prentice and me together. But what if he did? He'll tell Dave and Dave will tell Dad and I'll be grounded and never see Prentice again. Calm down. But I can't calm down—not when I feel so cornered, so trapped. "I've been skating." There, didn't that sound as if I had nothing to hide?

Larry nodded. "That's nice." His eyes slid away from mine.

He *had* seen us. If I beg him hard enough, will he keep my secret? Larry Woods—my brother's best friend—someone who'd always been in the background of my life, had suddenly stepped to the forefront and was standing between me and my true love. Why did he, of all people, have to take this particular bus on this particular afternoon? It wasn't fair. He shouldn't have done this to me.

The bus lurched to a stop to discharge an old man who used a cane to fumble his way to the curb. Larry slumped into the newly vacated seat and stared out the window. Something about the way he held his head, the set of his shoulders, caused my anger to change to puzzlement. I felt that whatever was on Larry's mind had nothing to do with Prentice and me.

Just to be on the safe side though, all the way home I practiced different ways of asking him not to say anything about what he might have seen. By the time we reached our stop, I thought I'd found the right words to make him understand how important Prentice was to me and how I hated sneaking out to meet him, but it was only because Dad was so strict and—

"You going to the game Friday night?" Larry asked as we started up Pringle Hill.

"If Ellen wants to," I replied. Ah, the solid ground of an everyday subject—the football rivalry with Hoover High. A chance to avoid the shifting sand of whether or not he'd seen me and Prentice together and whether or not he'd tell anyone.

"I hear Ellen might be leaving."

"Well, her dad's been transferred someplace else, but I hope she'll be able to stay with us for a while."

We exchanged a few more random sentences that meant nothing, then a cloud of silence settled between us. By the time we got to Guy Street, I knew I had to break through that silence. "Larry, did you . . . ?"

"I might as well tell you . . ." he said at the same moment. "Sorry. You go first."

"I was wondering if you saw who I was with just before I got on the bus."

"That marine? Sure."

"Well, that was Prentice and I met him at the skating rink and I like him a lot. Please do me a big favor and don't say anything to anyone. Please. It's really important to me."

Larry shrugged. "Why should I tell anyone? It's none of my business."

"I'm going to tell my folks about him, but you know Dad. I'm . . ."

"Like I said, it's not my business." With those curt words he dismissed me. Mixed with my relief was a curious disappointment that what had been so monumentally important to me was so trivial to him. We said so long to each other and he walked down the block toward his house. It wasn't until he was out of hearing range that I remembered he'd started to tell me something. Oh, well, I thought as I walked up the three steps to our front porch, I guess whatever it was can keep.

Chapter 6

Hand in hand, we were strolling barefoot along the moon-drenched beach. Wavelets lapped at the shore, pulled back, then washed forward again in an endless rhythm. Then he stopped, held me in a gentle embrace, and placed his lips upon mine. And we became a part of the rhythm of the night, for the moment unaware of time and of worldly demands, knowing only that we belonged together.

For at least the tenth time in an hour, I tried to concentrate on my math homework. It was no use. My mind was just too full of Prentice and all the other things that were going on in my life. First of all, I was again taking Japanese lessons from Mr. Narasaki and spending hours on my English-lit project. Second, Mrs. Hill was leaving at the end of the week and she had said that Ellen could stay with us until the semester was over, and miracle of miracles, Dad had said it was all right. Now I had only two days to get the old army cot out of the basement and set it up in my room and clear away some space in the closet and dresser for Ellen's things. I also had to talk Dad into taking Ellen's mother to the pier, but that was really no big problem. Dad was usually right there when someone needed something, even if that person was little more than a stranger.

With all the things that were going on, I hadn't found the chance to tell my folks about Prentice. The task loomed bigger and blacker with every day that passed.

I was still struggling with my math when the screen door slammed and Dave came into the dining room. He passed me without so much as a "Hi, kid," which to me was a signal that he had something weighty on his mind.

"What's going on?" I put down my pencil and stretched my arms over my head.

When Dave turned to face me, I saw that his hair was glistening with droplets of rain, that some of them were dripping onto his face, but he did nothing to wipe them away. "Larry just told me the navy rejected him—something about a heart murmur." Slumping into the chair opposite me, he stared at the floor. "He found out about it a few days ago, but . . . get this . . . he was so torn up about it he couldn't tell me about it until now." He got up and started pacing. "Me . . . his best friend and he couldn't tell me. That's how upset he was."

A fragment of thought skipped through my mind but was gone before I could grab hold of it. "I can't believe this. Larry's never been sick—never missed any school. He's even gone out for basketball." The fragment appeared again, and this time I knew what it was. "When did he get rejected?"

"Last Saturday, and he didn't even tell his parents until last night."

Saturday. "I might as well tell you," he said, but I'd never given him a chance to finish—just kept on about Prentice and my problems while he was going through what must be the biggest disappointment of his life.

But that's silly, I thought. He couldn't have been going to tell me. Why, he hadn't even said anything to his folks for three whole days. Well, it couldn't make any difference now. If Larry *had* felt like confiding in me, I'd been too preoccupied with my own problems to even listen to his.

During the next couple of days, the only time I saw Larry was when we passed in the hall at school—hardly the time to find out how he was taking his rejection. Meanwhile, I was being swept along on the tide of my own life. On Monday Dad and I went to Ellen's place to pick up her things and take them to our house, and on Tuesday I spent a couple of hours rearranging my room, which I'd already rearranged twice. Then on Wednesday morning while I was in school, Dad took Ellen and Mrs. Hill to the pier and waited around until they'd said their final good-byes. That afternoon, my mind was busy going over all the things we could do over the next few months. Ride the Coronado Ferry, go to the zoo, window-shop along Fifth Avenue. Maybe even do some real shopping, because Mrs. Hill had given Ellen a twenty-dollar bill for her expense money. A fortune, and yet Ellen had barely glanced at it as she tucked it away in her wallet. Me? I would have been jumping up and down, ecstatic with the realization that I could now buy the pair of skates I'd always coveted but at ten dollars had never been able to afford.

Skating. Prentice. What would he do when he found that I still hadn't told my parents? I pushed the thought aside. Surely, sometime during the next two days, I'd find a way to let them know.

By the time I got home Ellen had finished unpacking her suitcases and was helping Mom fold some sheets. "It's going to be nice having an extra pair of hands to help with the work around here," Mom said.

Ellen's smile looked forced, and she didn't say anything. Figuring a good laugh would make her feel at home, I said, "Knock, knock."

There was no answer from Ellen, so Mom said, "Who's there?"

"Artichokes."

"Artichokes who?" Mom replied.

" 'Artichokes any good?' said the Swede to the man who was listening to Fred Allen on the radio."

Mom laughed, but there was no sound from Ellen as she dropped her end of the sheet and ran into our bedroom.

"Better go see what's wrong," Mom said.

Ellen was sitting on the edge of my bed, her face buried in her hands. I stood near the door, confused, wavering. Should I put my arms around her, say some soothing words? But how could I comfort her when I didn't have the least idea as to why she was crying? "I know my jokes are bad, but . . ." I stopped, suddenly aware that it was better to be quiet than to say the wrong thing.

Ellen raised her tear-streaked face to look at me. "I . . . I m-miss Mom. I should have gone with her."

"But . . . but . . ." Had it all been for nothing—all the trouble I'd gone to so she could stay here—getting Dad's permission—digging around in our dusty, cobwebby basement to find that cot—moving everything in my room so we'd both fit into it? All that work and worry just so Ellen could sit here and say she'd changed her mind?

I guess the worst part was that we were supposed to be best friends, and I'd thought she'd want to be with me as much as I wanted her here. I felt unappreciated, almost betrayed, until an almost-forgotten moment in my life flashed into my consciousness. I was eight years old, and tears rolled down my cheeks as I sat on a large rock watching the dust kicked up by my parents' Essex.

The car disappeared, hidden by a clump of trees, and I was abandoned, left in the hands of strangers. It made no difference that I had pleaded for a chance to spend a week at Brownie camp. They shouldn't have listened to me. They should have said no.

Did Ellen wish that her mother had insisted on her going to Honolulu? I put my hand on her shoulder. "Please don't cry. Just think about all the good times we're going to have . . . and don't forget you'll be able to keep on seeing Jack. You wouldn't be able to do that if you'd left."

Ellen wiped her eyes with the edge of the bedspread. "I know. I know. I'll be all right. But I can't help thinking about . . ." She took a deep shuddery breath. "About Mom waving good-bye. For a minute I had this awful feeling that something bad was going to happen to her."

"Nothing bad's going to happen. I guarantee it."

"Maybe it's because . . . well, Mom and I have always been together, even though Dad's been gone a lot. I'm sorry I'm acting like this. It's dumb."

I picked up one of Ellen's suitcases and put it in the closet. "No, it's not. I think I know how you feel. It's okay."

But deep inside of me, I was vaguely disturbed. There had been so many times when I'd wished that Ellen would share her feelings with me, but now that she had, the experience had been unsettling, and I had handled it badly, had fallen short of being the understanding, compassionate friend I wanted to be.

By the next day, Ellen, in her usual practical way, seemed to have accepted the fact that there were some benefits to staying in San Diego. That afternoon on the way home from school, every outward trace of her homesickness had disappeared. As the streetcar lumbered up to the plaza, she crossed her fingers and looked upward. "Please, please, don't let Jack and Prentice get shipped out, and let them get passes tomorrow."

Tomorrow. I gritted my teeth. By tomorrow there'd be only a few more hours in which to make good on the promise I'd made to Prentice. "What am I going to say when I see Prentice?" I lowered my voice, reluctant to share my misery with the other bus passengers. "He meant what he said . . . I just know it."

"Tonight, right after dinner, you're going to sit your father down and let him know everything. After all, you haven't done anything wrong."

"It isn't that easy. You don't know Dad like I do. He's likely to ground me forever."

Ellen didn't say anything for a few moments, but her eyes got a faraway look in them and her lips were pressed together—signs that her mind was going full speed ahead. "Maybe . . . oh, it probably wouldn't work. Forget it."

"What? Come on. Tell me."

"Do you suppose . . . well, do you think your folks would let Jack and Prentice come up for dinner sometime?"

She hadn't been listening to me at all! "How can you ask me something like that when . . . ?" When I raised my voice, the elderly woman sitting in front of us turned her head, and I saw the disapproval in her eyes. Chastened, I looked out the window for a moment, and during that moment my spirits began to soar. Ellen was right! There had to be a way to get permission to have Prentice and Jack come to the house—after all, that wasn't like a date, it was just having company over, and when Mom and Dad saw how nice Prentice is—my heart started to race. This plan could work. It really could.

Our stop was coming up, so I raised my arm and pulled the buzzer cord. Flashing my bus pass at the driver, I followed Ellen out onto the curb. "Well?" she said.

"It won't hurt to ask, right? I'll do it tonight . . . after dinner." How wonderful it will be—me serving Prentice a home-cooked meal, him smiling his appreciation as he savors the first succulent bite, the radio playing romantic music in the background. Candles, yes, we must have candles, and flowers as a centerpiece. Bits of lacy fern, pansies, honeysuckle. It will all be so perfect. I can't wait. I can't wait.

Chapter 7

*T*HE END JUSTIFIES THE MEANS—THAT'S WHAT I KEPT TELLING myself to quiet my nagging conscience. Tonight—right after the news broadcast was over—that's the time that Ellen and I had set to act out our carefully prepared script. And now the hour had arrived, and I wasn't ready, was unwilling, to recite my lines. When Ellen glanced my way, I shook my head slightly, but she either didn't see that I had changed my mind, or she chose to ignore it.

"Jack's going to be shipped out soon," she said.

"Oh?" Mom replied. "Jack . . . he's the boy from the skating rink, isn't he?"

Ellen nodded as she waited for me to carry out my part in the well-rehearsed dialogue. When I didn't, she went ahead by herself. "That's right. And you know what? He said his only wish is that he have one more home-cooked dinner before he leaves." She glanced at me. "Didn't you say he has a friend who has the same wish? Prentice . . . wasn't that his name?"

Prentice—I'd made him a promise, and while this wasn't a chance to completely fulfill that promise, it *was* a way to get him up here to meet Mom and Dad and to help Ellen out, too. It's true, I thought, the end *does* justify the means. "Yes, Prentice.

He *did* say something about how awful the mess hall food is." I braced myself for Dad's objections. They weren't long in coming.

"I knew no good would come of your spending all that time at the skating rink. Two young girls with all those sailors and marines. Now, look what's happened." He glared at Ellen. "What would your mother think of this? I . . ."

"John!" The sharp tone of Mom's voice startled me—and Dad, too, judging by the way his voice faded away and his shocked expression as he turned his head to look at her. "You should be pleased that the girls want to entertain their friends at home, that they aren't sneaking around behind our backs. And how can we say no to two homesick servicemen? A home-cooked meal is little enough for them to ask, considering . . ."

Dad's face was flushed as he opened his mouth to respond to Mom's attack, and I cringed, expecting a full-blown counter-offensive. Then I saw Dad's Adam's apple move up and down, as though he was swallowing his pride. "We'll talk about this later, Dorothy," he said, his voice low and even.

I put my silverware on my empty plate and picked up my glass. Just before I stood up to carry them into the kitchen, I felt a gentle nudge on my ankle. When I looked at Dave, he winked at me. While I appreciated his quiet show of support, right now I wanted nothing more than to be alone to await Mom and Dad's decision. For a moment, I wondered if I wouldn't have been better off if I'd never met Prentice. That feeling passed as quickly as it had appeared, but as I scraped the dishes and put away the leftovers, an unsettling guilt welled up inside of me. "They're not sneaking around behind our backs," Mom had said, defiance flashing from her eyes. How betrayed she would feel if she knew about those long talks I'd had with Prentice, how I'd held his hand, about those dreams that crept into my sleep and that whispered to me when I was awake, about the invisible but indelible imprint that had been left when his lips had brushed my cheek.

Ellen came into the kitchen, picked up a dishtowel, and started drying as I washed. "What do you think?" she said in a half-whisper. "Will they say yes?"

I shrugged and shook my head, my sense of guilt tinged with a resentment that it was her idea that had caused my mother to lash out at my father, humbling him in front of Dave and me. I'd often wished that Mom would speak her mind; now that she had, it made me uneasy.

I don't know what transpired between my parents that evening, but the next morning Mom said that we could have our company for dinner the following Sunday.

"Your father set down just one condition," Mom said. "He says that you girls are to do all the shopping and cooking and cleaning."

At the time, that had seemed little enough to ask. Besides, Ellen said between the two of us we could certainly prepare a meal that would compare favorably with mess hall food. Her show of confidence led me to assume she knew a lot more about cooking than I did.

By 4:15 on Sunday afternoon, as I attacked the potatoes with a masher, my own confidence was being slowly undermined. Gone was my vision of a perfectly set table laden with steaming food that looked like the pictures in *Ladies Home Companion*; of my greeting Prentice with every hair in place, looking like a model in the Montgomery Ward catalog. In its place was the growing knowledge that the afternoon was going to be a disaster to rival that of the sinking of the *Titanic*.

"Look at these lumps," I moaned. "They're *never* going to come out."

Ellen frowned as she peered into the pan. "Maybe it needs more milk or butter or something."

"If I put anything else in there, we'll end up with potato soup." I wiped my forehead with the edge of the dishtowel. "Hey, what's all that smoke? The pork chops! They're burning up!"

"Oh, my gosh!" Ellen ran to the stove, grabbed a fork, and turned the meat. "Well, I don't think they're exactly ruined . . . just a little well done on one side."

"Do you think we should put the string beans on now?" Even in the midst of my growing panic, my conscience was telling me that I was about to pay for not telling Mom the entire truth.

"Probably," Ellen said. "I'm not sure how long they're supposed to cook, but if they get done too fast, we can always warm them up." As she turned the fire on under the pot, I looked at the wall clock above the stove. Forty more minutes and Jack and Prentice will be here and the table isn't even set yet! Oh, please God, let everything turn out all right . . . if you do I'll never do anything wrong again as long as I live. . . .

I took a deep breath, hoping that God hadn't been too busy to hear my promise, then realized that He was probably using this afternoon as a way to punish me for my collective sins. "We should have known we couldn't do all this by ourselves," I said.

"It'll turn out all right." Ellen opened the backdoor and waved some of the smoke out with a towel. "But getting a whole dinner together sure isn't like making a snickerdoodle in cooking class."

I groaned. "Look, the potatoes are turning *gray*! Oh, my gosh, the rolls. We forgot about the rolls!"

The oven wasn't preheated when I slid the tray in, but I figured we could just cook the rolls a little longer to make up for it. There were footsteps on the back stairs, and a second later, Dave was standing in the doorway, grinning like a chimpanzee with a fist full of peanuts. "Did you remember to lay in a supply of bicarb?" he said.

I threw a pot holder at him. "No one's going to get indigestion." My mouth said the words, but my good sense told me different. Tonight Prentice will have the biggest stomachache of his entire life and he'll never speak to me again.

My nerves tensed up another notch when Ellen turned down the fire under the pork chops and announced that she was going to change her dress. "But you can't . . . not yet. You're supposed to fix the gravy," I wailed.

"I'll just be a minute," she called before she shut our bedroom door after her.

"Dave, what am I going to do? Look at this mess." I peeked at the string beans and almost surrendered to the tears of frustration that had been dammed up inside me. The water had barely started to boil, and the beans were just sitting there, doing absolutely nothing. "Prentice will never want to see me again."

I gritted my teeth, tensed my shoulders, restrained myself from clapping my hand over my mouth. Prentice was supposed to be nothing more than a casual acquaintance—someone I'd skated with a few times. If that were true, Dave must be wondering why I was so worried about his opinion of my culinary abilities.

It was hard to tell what Dave was thinking, because he was looking at the potatoes and making a face. "What in the dickens . . . ?"

"I'll take care of it." My voice was snappy, not because of his criticism, but because I knew his comment was well founded. "After I do all the stuff that Ellen's supposed to be doing . . . fix the gravy, set the table."

"Hey, I can do the gravy. I've watched Mom stir it up hundreds of times."

If he wouldn't have thought I was crazy, I would have hugged him. I just wasn't up to facing that yucky black stuff in the bottom of the frying pan and trying to turn it into anything edible. "Thanks," I said, not knowing whether he was a gravy expert or not, but more than willing to let him take the blame or the praise for the results.

While Dave stirred and sifted, I put the extra leaf in the dining-room table, then unfolded our linen tablecloth, the one we use for special occasions like holidays. I had just finished smoothing it down when I heard footsteps on the front porch. My heart lurched. Were they here already? But it wasn't time. I started toward my room, calling to Dave to answer the door, frantically yanking the curlers and pins out of my hair, hating Ellen when she walked out of our bedroom looking cool and composed in her starched white blouse and green dirndl skirt and her hair brushed smooth and shiny and tied back with a ribbon like an Ivory soap girl, while I must have looked like Frankenstein's sister with my curls popping out from my head like corkscrews.

"Are they here?" Ellen asked. "I heard someone." Before I had a chance to say a word, she walked into the front room and put her hand on the doorknob. Wait! I wanted to shout. Don't open it until . . . But it was only Mom and Dad returning from the walk they had taken because, as Mom said, she couldn't stand by and watch her kitchen being demolished.

"I think your company will be here soon," Mom said. "There's a sailor and a marine coming up the hill." She peeked into the kitchen. "Whew, what a mess. And what did you burn? I could smell it almost all the way to the corner."

"Oh, Mom, would you . . . ?"

My voice must have sounded as distraught as I felt, because Mom smiled, put her hand on my back, and pushed me toward my room. "You go get ready. Ellen can finish setting the table while I salvage what's left of the meal."

"Hope it won't take too long." Dad sounded grumpy. He never liked to have his schedule disrupted, but at this point I didn't give a fig for being the cause of his bad mood. My own personal debacle-in-the-making took precedence over whatever inconvenience he was experiencing.

I bolted for my room, pulled my apron over my head, shuffled through the clothes in my closet, looking for my pink princess-style dress. My jacket and one of Ellen's blouses slid off their hangers and tumbled to the floor, and I left them lying there in a heap. No time to pick them up. No time to . . .

And then I heard the muffled buzz of the doorbell, the sound of Dad's footsteps across the carpet, the creak of the screen door as it opened, then closed. He was here! Right in my house! My hands trembled as I fought to get the zipper of my dress unstuck. How would I ever be able to eat with him sitting there at the table?

The door opened and Ellen poked her head into the room. "It's them," she whispered. "You almost ready?"

That was a dumb question, because she could see that I had barely started brushing out my curls. "I'm going as fast as I can," I said. "Go talk to them."

Even though I'd put up my hair following the directions for a pageboy in a magazine, the ends just wouldn't go under. Well, at least it wasn't lopsided or fuzzy. After giving it a final stroke with the brush, I pinched my cheeks to make them glow, stood up, took a deep breath, closed my eyes, and counted to five, then opened the door.

Dad was sitting in his big upholstered chair in the front room and Jack and Prentice were on opposite ends of the couch while

Ellen was perched on the edge of the occasional chair. There was no place for me, unless I plopped myself down on the couch between the guys, and I couldn't do that. Being that close to Prentice with Dad right there in the room with us—well, I just couldn't, so I pulled up a dining-room chair. Please don't let Dave call me kid, I prayed. Please let Dad like Prentice. Please let the pork chops be all right. Please don't let me spill gravy on my dress.

". . . and as far as I'm concerned, we should keep our noses out of European affairs, and that goes for China, too," Dad was saying.

"Maybe so," Jack said. "But there comes a time when you have to stick up for your friends."

Dad held up his index finger. "Ah, but first you have to know who your real friends are. You know that politics make strange bedfellows."

I'd heard that saying, and I had no idea what it meant, and I wished that Dad would talk about something else. "I'll go see about dinner," I said. "I guess everyone must be starving." I hoped my voice wasn't as trembly as it sounded to me.

"Something sure smells good," Prentice said as I left the room. To me, the air was still filled with the smell of burnt meat.

I don't know what sort of magic Dave and Mom had done, but by the time everyone sat down at the table, the potatoes were lump-free, the gravy was smooth and didn't taste burnt at all, and the string beans were tender and buttery. My stomach was so knotted up that I could only pick at the food, but Prentice and Jack ate big helpings of everything.

During the first part of dinner I just kept quiet and let the talk swirl around me. "So you're from Minnesota," Dad said to Prentice. "Must be a lot of snow there this time of year. I bet you don't miss that one little bit."

Prentice shook his head. "Well, it may sound funny, but I do. There's nothing like a white Christmas."

"Well, you have a right to your opinion." Dad buttered a roll and glanced at his watch. Oh, no, I thought. You're not going to listen to the news tonight—not when we have company. But he did. At a few minutes after six, the room was filled with the sound of Gabriel Heatter's voice. ". . . and plans are being made in Washington to welcome the Japanese emissaries. Many high-level government officials are doubtful that the talks will do much good, however. They say that the Japanese will insist on the lifting of embargoes and the unfreezing of their assets in this country, concessions that President Roosevelt shows no signs of granting. Meanwhile, Secretary of State Cordell Hull . . ."

"Oh, my gosh!" Ellen got up so fast she almost knocked her chair over. "We forgot the salad." She rushed into the kitchen and returned carrying a large cut glass bowl.

Prentice smiled his wonderful slow smile and my heart almost stopped. "Waldorf. My favorite. Mom makes it all the time."

Say something, dummy, I said to myself, or Mom will sure know there's something wrong here. "We usually just have it on holidays." Not much of a conversation stopper, but better than nothing.

Dad turned the radio up. "Seems that with you boys being in the service, you'd want to know what's going on in the world."

"Only two of us are in the service, Dad," Dave said. "Just say the word though, and we can make it three."

Dave, please don't, not tonight, I pleaded silently, willing him to be quiet just this once.

"Save room for some strawberry ice cream." There was Mom, smoothing things over again. "Dad and I picked it up at the Orchid."

"Boy, talk about favorites . . . strawberry ice cream is mine."
Jack rubbed his stomach. "You sure spread a good table, ma'am."

Mom smiled. "But the girls did all the work."

"Yep, my Marjorie will make some lucky guy a great little wife
someday." Dad had turned the radio down during a commercial
and his words rolled around the room like the pealing of a bell in
a church tower. How could he do that? As far as he knew, Prentice
and I were little more than strangers and there he was talking
about *marriage*, of all things. Oh, why can't I just slither under
the table and crawl off somewhere? Never again will I go along
with anything Ellen suggests—just look at her there, laughing
and talking just as if everything was going along perfectly. Doesn't
she realize that my world is collapsing around my ears? Some
friend—and then I tuned in on what Dad was saying to Jack. "So,
you have any idea of where you'll be heading when you get those
orders?"

"It's hard to say," Jack replied. "If I believe the scuttlebutt,
it'll be the Philippines, but that's going to be a while yet."

And we had said the reason for this dinner was that Jack was
leaving soon. What was that old saying? Hoisted on your own
petard? That's what had happened all right.

I got up and started collecting the dinner plates, trying to avoid
Mom's questioning eyes, not able to look at Prentice, because if
I did my hands would shake and I'd drop something. "Anyone
ready for dessert?" My voice sounded tight, unnatural.

"Sure enough," Prentice said. I glanced at him and felt the
blood rush to my face.

Mom got up, too. "I'll get Dad his coffee. Do you boys want
some?"

Both of them shook their heads. I was glad because Dad always
said that coffee was a grown-up drink, that it would stunt your

growth if you drank it before you were twenty-one. I didn't think Prentice had to worry about that, since he was already five-foot-ten.

I followed Mom into the kitchen. She got the ice cream out while I took the dessert dishes from the cupboard. "Prentice seems like a nice boy," she said, her voice almost too casual.

"He is, and he's a good skater, too."

As Mom handed me two dishes of ice cream, her eyes met mine. Deep inside of them, there was a suspicion—no, more than that —an awareness. How stupid I'd been to think I could keep the truth from her when everything I'd done today, every movement I'd made, every word I'd spoken must have told her Prentice was much more than just one of Jack's friends.

"Mom . . ." I hesitated, trying to find the right words. "Mom, thanks for letting him come to dinner. I like him. I like him a lot."

Her eyes softened. "I thought so. Go on now . . . the ice cream's melting. We can talk more about this later."

As I walked back into the dining room, I wondered whether or not anyone could tell that my feet weren't touching the floor. Mom knew—she *knew*—and there had been no tensing of her jaw, no frown. Maybe she remembered what it was like to be young and in love; maybe she could imagine what it was like to have time pressing in, to have to live with the knowledge that these few hours, these precious moments, might be the last we'd ever have together.

Maybe someday I'd be able to thank her for giving me this afternoon, one that I was suddenly sure I'd number among the best afternoons of my life.

Chapter 8

*I*T HAD HAPPENED AGAIN—ELLEN HAD PUSHED SOME OF HER clothes onto my side of the closet. I shoved them back, seething as I thought about all the times she'd thrown her dirty socks on my bed, used my notebook paper without asking, and dumped her shoes by the door right where I kept stumbling over them. Boy, living with someone was sure a lot different from just eating lunch or going someplace on the weekend with them.

The surge of annoyance disappeared as fast as it had appeared. It was Saturday, after all, and nothing mattered except the fact that in a little over an hour I'd be skating with Prentice again. And today was even more special because Mom and Dad knew all about us, so Prentice would no longer be wrestling with his conscience. Of course, neither would I, although I was still a little perplexed about Dad's proclamation—"Just as long as you come right home afterward . . . don't get any ideas about doing anything else."

Now, exactly what had he meant by "anything else"? A movie maybe? (Oh, to sit in the cool darkness holding hands, shoulders touching, all the way through a double feature, a cartoon, and a newsreel) or going to the zoo (then strolling through Balboa Park, stealing a quick kiss when no one was looking).

Ellen came into the room, kicked off her slippers, and kneeled on the floor to look under my bed. "You almost ready?" she asked.

"Yep. Just have to find my jacket. By the way, if you're looking for your shoes, I put them in the corner."

"Oh, thanks. And your jacket's on the shelf. I needed the hanger."

"Well, you're welcome, I'm sure." My voice reflected sarcasm, but Ellen didn't seem to notice. "I wish . . . hey, where the heck's my brush?"

"Oh, in the bathroom. I couldn't find mine, so I borrowed it."

Holding back a stream of angry words, I stalked out of the room. We really were going to have to have a little talk, but not today, not when Prentice might even now be boarding a bus, heading toward downtown and the Skating Palace, his hand anticipating my touch, his eyes longing to look into mine, his lips . . .

"Hey, it's almost one-fifteen," Ellen called after me. "Hurry up, or we'll miss the bus. You shouldn't have stayed so long at Kaye's."

So now it was Kaye's fault that we were late. Ellen never missed a chance to let me know she didn't like the Narasakis. Thank goodness Dad understood how important my English-lit project was.

As we half ran down the hill, the clouds were gathering over Point Loma, and by the time the bus came, a light rain was dotting the sidewalk. Ellen didn't say much on the way downtown, and that was fine with me because I was busy thinking about touching the rough texture of Prentice's uniform jacket and inhaling its woolly smell and drowning in the sight of his sweet smile and the sound of his drawly voice.

We got off the bus and headed toward the skating rink, dodging men and women with umbrellas and pretending to ignore the occasional wolf whistles and stares from the sailors and marines who were leaning on lampposts and gathered on corners. I tried to save the little bit of curl I had left by pulling up the hood of my jacket, while Ellen put a bandanna over her head and tied it under her chin.

"I was hoping the rain would hold off till tonight," I said, more to break the silence than anything else.

"It doesn't make any difference to me." Ellen's voice was so low I could barely hear it above the swish of tires on the damp street. "I have this awful feeling that Jack won't show up this afternoon. He's been shipped out. I know he has."

"You had the feeling that something bad was going to happen to your mother when she left for Honolulu," I said. "And there she is doing just fine. Couldn't it be that your crystal ball needs fixing?" When I saw the desolate look in her eyes, I turned off the sarcasm. "If he'd had to leave, he would have found a way to let you know."

"Sometimes they don't have time to make any phone calls. That happened to Dad once. Mom almost went crazy before she heard from him."

"Just wait. He'll be at the rink, I promise." My assurances sounded hollow, even to my ears. Shipped out. Lots of guys had told me they were going to be shipped out, but before I met Prentice the words hadn't held any special meaning for me. A cold knot formed in my chest. Someday—some terrible day—time would run out and Prentice would leave San Diego, leaving me behind, waiting, hoping, praying, living through all those empty weeks and months.

If Ellen's premonition came true, that's what she was facing right now. I gave myself a mental slap for being so upset with her this morning.

Prentice was waiting just inside the door of the skating rink. "Hi," I said, and the joy that bubbled up inside of me left little room for Ellen's dark forebodings. "Hi," he answered, and the aroma of his witch hazel made me light-headed, glad I couldn't see into the future. Right now, at this moment, we were together. Nothing else mattered.

It wasn't until Prentice had finished lacing up my skates that I saw that Ellen was still standing by the entrance of the rink, her face pinched, her eyes wide as they glanced at, then discarded, each sailor that passed by. None of them was Jack, and I wanted to run to her, to tell her I was no stranger to her agony, because that's how I had felt when Prentice was late.

I took Prentice's hand, but instead of following him into the skating area, I hesitated. "Ellen's worried about Jack," I said. "Maybe I should go see if I can help."

"Sure. You go ahead. I'll wait here."

"It will be all right," I was going to say to her. "Just have faith and you'll find that everything for which you yearn will be yours. Faith can move mountains. Faith will give you the strength to . . ."

Well, that's what a priest had said to someone in a movie I saw a while ago. Somehow, I didn't think it would sound the same coming from me. I'd just stand beside her, tell her I understand . . . but wait, Ellen's face had lit up like a hundred-watt bulb and there was Jack, reaching out to take her hands in his.

Prentice stood up as I skated back to him. "Looks like we don't have to worry about your friend anymore," he said. "Let's get out there and enjoy the music."

"Right." How happy I was for Ellen, but I was even more happy for me. The organist was playing a waltz, and the slow rhythm swept us around the rink as we moved together in effortless precision. The morning and its petty irritations were now a part of what seemed to be a distant past. Five o'clock lay far in the future.

But then the music stopped, and I was aware of loud laughter, the smell of dust in the air, the whir and clunk of metal wheels contacting the floor. I was also aware that something was wrong with Jack and Ellen. They were still standing at the front of the rink, their faces close, unsmiling.

When fifteen minutes more had passed and Jack hadn't headed for the skate rental counter, I couldn't ignore my rising apprehension. "Guess I better see what's going on with Ellen," I said, wanting Prentice to tell me to leave her alone, to insist that I not take the chance of letting anything intrude upon these magical moments.

But, as I knew he would, he nodded his head and released my hand. "Guess you'd better. I'll wait here."

As I skated up to Jack and Ellen, my question was answered before I had a chance to ask it. "I got my orders," Jack said. "My ship's pulling out of Dago next Friday."

I forced myself to look at Ellen while groping for a soothing phrase that would melt the cold bleakness of her expression. But there was no such group of healing words. "I'm sorry" was all I could come up with, stunned as I was with the near-accuracy of her prediction.

Her mother's gone, and now Jack. What will she do? That thought had barely skipped through my head when it was replaced by another. What will *I* do when Prentice leaves? Because he *is* going to leave, there's no doubt about that. So what will I do when all I have left is the hope that someday we'll be together again?

I pushed the unanswerable questions away from me. Whatever may happen in the future had nothing to do with the fact that Ellen needed me right now.

"Do you want to go someplace else?" I asked. "We could . . ."

Ellen shook her head. "No, it's all right. You two go ahead and skate. We're going for a walk. See you later."

Neither Prentice nor I said much as we continued skating. Maybe he was thinking, as I was, about what was going to happen when he got his orders.

On that cold, dreary day, the memories had been almost too much to bear. To find some comfort, I was riding the Coronado Ferry, looking at the horizon, letting the sea breeze ruffle my perfumed hair, so lost in reverie that I was only dimly aware of the sailor who had joined me at the railing.

"You alone, miss?" His voice was deep and strangely soothing. I nodded.

"I, too, am alone," he said. "Perhaps we can share our loneliness."

"I am alone, but I am not lonely," I murmured. "My marine is with me in spirit."

"I understand." The sailor's gaze was soft, yet penetrating.

My heart ached as he walked away, swaying in response to the movement of the ferry. He needed someone, but I was too deeply engrossed in my memories to meet that need.

"Hey, you look like you're a hundred miles away," Prentice said. "This thing with Ellen really has you upset, doesn't it?"

I nodded, too full of a jumble of sadness and longing and contentment and joy to answer him.

Ellen and Jack didn't come back to the rink, and there was no sign of them at the plaza as Prentice and I waited for my bus. I worried about her all the way home, but knew there was nothing to do except be there for her when she showed up.

The rain had eased into a steady drizzle by the time I turned onto our street, but there was Larry sitting on our front-porch steps. "You're getting soaked," I said. "Come on inside."

"Naw, it's all right. Dave'll be out in a second." He moved over to let me pass. Instead, I sat beside him. For a few moments we said nothing. The only sounds came from an occasional passing car and the foghorn in the bay.

"Haven't seen much of you lately."

"Been busy." Larry ran his fingers through his hair. "Thinking about college and stuff."

"Well, that's one good thing about not going in the service. You'll be able to stay in school." My lips twitched. "My gosh, I sound like Dad, don't I?"

Larry frowned and shook his head. "Please don't talk about that."

"What? School?" But even as I asked the question, I knew I'd made a hurtful blunder. Hadn't Dave told me that Larry was still stinging from his rejection? Why had I brought it up? While I was fumbling for something to direct his attention away from the distasteful subject, Dave opened the front door and stepped onto the porch.

Larry stood up. "Take care, Marj. Hey, I hear you had a bang-up dinner party the other day. Your cooking must have improved since the last time I sampled it."

I laughed. "It hasn't. If it hadn't been for Dave and Mom, the meal would have been a complete flop."

"What's a brother for anyway?" Dave called over his shoulder as he and Larry walked toward Pringle Hill, two good friends chuckling over some secret joke. And where's *my* friend? I wondered, suddenly aware that my vague uneasiness had sharpened into anxiety. Ellen, let me know what's happening. I want to help you.

I must have made at least ten trips to the corner to look for Ellen before Mom decided we might as well go ahead and eat dinner. While I picked at my food, Dad kept glancing at his watch and exchanging worried looks with Mom. After I washed and dried the dishes, I walked to the corner again, but there still no sign of Ellen.

"Maybe I should take the car and go look for her," Dad said a few minutes later.

"But where would you start?" Mom asked. "She could be anyplace."

"Anything's better than just sitting around," I said. "She and Jack might be at the hamburger place there at Second and Broadway. Or they could just be walking around the plaza. We could . . ."

There was the welcome sound of footsteps on the porch, then the squeak of the screen door opening. A second later Ellen was standing in the front room, shivering, her hair plastered to her head. I put my arms around her, relief sweeping through me like a soothing balm, unraveling the knots in my stomach.

Mom helped Ellen peel off her jacket. "Goodness, you're going to catch your death of cold, and then what would your mother think of the way we watch over you? March yourself into the bedroom and change your clothes. I'll fix you some cinnamon toast and hot chocolate."

Cinnamon toast and hot chocolate—Mom's long-standing remedy for almost every human ailment from stomachache to heartache.

"You've had us mighty worried, young lady." Dad's voice was

gruff, but his expression was that of gentle concern. "What have you got to say for yourself?"

"Now, you just leave her alone, John," Mom said as she guided Ellen toward our room. "She can give her explanations later when she's warm and dry."

I followed Ellen to the bedroom, then shut the door. "Are you all right? Where did you go? What did you talk about? I've been so worried!"

Ellen took off her blouse and skirt, dumped them on the floor, and put on her limp chenille robe. "I know, I know. And I'm sorry, but Jack and I . . . it was just like nothing else mattered."

"Well, sure, but . . ."

"I've decided to go to Honolulu."

"What?" I had heard the words, but my mind refused to accept them.

"I'm going to ask Mom to send me a steamship ticket."

There were several seconds of silence, during which I tried to digest what she had said. I pulled back involuntarily when Ellen put her hand on my arm. "But what about all our plans? Thanksgiving vacation . . . Christmas . . ."

Tears trembled on her eyelashes. "I'm sorry, but I'm so homesick for Mom and I don't think I could stand it here without Jack." She brushed the tears away with the back of her hand. "Don't get me wrong. I've loved staying here, but . . . well, now that Jack's going there's not much reason to—"

"Not much reason!" My sense of betrayal found a voice. "We're best friends, for gosh sakes. Isn't that enough reason?"

Ellen reached out to touch my shoulder, but I backed away from her. She stood up and walked across the room, then turned to face me. "I could ask you the same thing. Admit it—one of the reasons you wanted me to stay here was so you'd have someone to go skating with. That way, you could go on seeing Prentice."

"No, no, I . . ." But wasn't she right? Deep down inside of me, when I had invited her, hadn't I been thinking as much of Prentice as I had of her? So she had used me and I had used her. Well, maybe that's part of being friends.

There was a light tapping on the door. "The chocolate's ready," Mom called. "And I fixed some eggs to go with the toast. Come on before everything gets cold."

I stood up. "I'm sorry. Everything's happening too fast for my feeble brain to take it all in." Taking her hand, I said, "Friends?"

"Friends. I'm going to miss you a lot." A half-smile flitted across her face. "But, hey, with the navy the way it is, I could be back in San Diego before you know it."

"And with the navy the way it is, Jack could be stationed at Pearl Harbor and you could come home from school some afternoon and there he'll be, sitting on your front steps waiting for you."

Ellen laughed. "Jack and I talked about that. It could happen, couldn't it?"

I just missed stepping on Ellen's blouse and slacks lying in a damp heap in the middle of the floor. Stooping to pick them up, I thought about how just this morning I'd been grumbling about all the mess she made, and now it didn't matter at all. My room was going to be a little neater when she was gone, but I was sure going to miss that giggling we did after the lights were out and we were supposed to be going to sleep.

I sighed. I'm going to miss a lot of things. How many weeks, how many months will pass before I see Ellen again?

Chapter 9

WHEN ELLEN FIRST CAME TO STAY WITH US, IT HAD SEEMED that we had been granted an endless supply of time—Saturday afternoons of skating, Sundays at the zoo, evenings during which we could listen to the radio and play records on our Victrola. But suddenly the time was gone, because Ellen's mother hadn't wasted a minute in sending the steamship ticket, air mail, even special delivery. There it was, lying in plain sight on my desk, a constant reminder that Ellen was leaving tomorrow, Thursday, at 9:30 in the morning.

I had to talk fast and furiously to get Dad to let me see Ellen off. At first he said absolutely not, but I kept after him until he backed down and said okay, as long as I went straight to school afterward. When the time came to go, though, I was wondering if I would have been better off if he'd said no. There we were, all crammed into the front seat of the car because the backseat was filled with boxes and suitcases, and the car wouldn't start. Again and again Dad turned the ignition key and pumped the gas pedal. Again and again the engine coughed and sputtered, then died.

"Damn!" he said, looking at his watch. "It's eight-thirty. We should be at the pier by now." Mom would have been upset if she had heard him swear in front of us. The worst she ever said when she had reached the end of her rope was "darn."

The next time Dad made an attempt, the smell of gasoline filled the car. "Great, just great. It's flooded." He pounded his fist on the steering wheel.

We sat there, wedged in tight, for about five more minutes. My left leg was going to sleep and my right arm ached from being pushed against the door handle. Ellen didn't complain, but I knew she must have felt squashed between Dad and me. Finally, though, Dad turned the key again, and after gasping a couple of times, the engine roared into action. Dad moved the gearshift, banging Ellen in the knee, and we started pulling away from the curb. Just then, Mom came running down the porch steps. "Wait!" she called. "Wait up!"

Dad's face turned red as he rolled the window down. "What now?"

Mom handed him a bulging paper sack. "Here's some sandwiches for Ellen, and a couple of apples, too."

"Good heavens, woman," Dad said. "Do you think they're going to let her starve on that ship?"

"It doesn't hurt to have a little something extra." Mom reached over Dad's chest and grabbed Ellen's hand. "Take good care of yourself, dear. We'll miss you."

"Thanks for everything," Ellen said. "I'll miss you, too."

"Say hello to your mother, and come back soon," Mom called as Dad let the car roll forward.

Neither Ellen nor I said anything as we went down Pringle Hill. I could feel tears pushing forward, and Ellen's eyes had a suspicious shine to them also. How fast the past year had gone, slipping almost unnoticed through our fingers, minute by minute, second by second. Looking forward, time seems so endless. Looking backward, six months is nothing more than the blink of an eye.

"I'll write every single day," Ellen said.

"Me, too."

Dad turned left onto Pacific Coast Highway. The fog was so thick we could barely see a half-block ahead, and the traffic was creeping along. That was all right with me, because I wasn't anxious to see Ellen board that steamship.

"Maybe you could get a job baby-sitting or something. Save your money, then come to see me in Honolulu," said Ellen.

At twenty-five cents an hour, it would take me a while to save up enough for my fare, but I was willing to try. The problem was that Dad didn't want me going into strange homes to work for people he'd never met. The fact that every other girl my age was allowed to baby-sit didn't make any difference. "Or maybe I could spend the summer clerking in a five-and-dime," I replied. I knew that later Dad would express his opinion of my getting a job and also of my going to Honolulu by myself. Knowing how tightly he liked to keep me reined, both ideas were beyond the realm of possibility.

Dad turned into a parking place near the B Street pier. "What sort of ship is your father assigned to?" he asked.

"A battleship. It's called . . . gee, I can't remember . . . some state . . . oh, yes, the *Arizona*, that's it."

"How exciting . . . a battleship," I said. "Maybe you'll be able to go on it someday."

"It could happen. Sometimes they let the families of the crew eat in the mess hall. I did that once when we were in Seattle. It was great . . . all those sailors looking at me when I walked up the gangplank. I was really dressed up, so I don't think they knew I was only thirteen."

I started to giggle, but cut it short when Dad gave me one of his looks. According to him, I wasn't supposed to like it when a serviceman looked at me. But can I help it if I'm walking down Broadway and I get a bunch of whistles that make me feel like Lana Turner must feel when she makes a personal appearance?

Dad went to get a cart so he could load up Ellen's luggage. Ellen and I just stood and looked at each other for a minute. "I can't believe you're really going," I said.

"I know what you mean." Ellen took my hand. "Good luck with Prentice."

"Same for you and Jack."

"Marjorie, I've never had as much fun anywhere as I've had with you."

"Same here." Tears welled up in my eyes.

We both looked at the liner that was going to carry her across the ocean. "Huge, isn't it?" Ellen said. "I wonder how I'll ever find my cabin."

"I guess they have people to show you around. In the movies they're always good-looking boys in cute uniforms."

"Well, I wouldn't mind that at all, but of course, I won't flirt because of Jack."

"Remember every single thing about your trip so you can write and tell me about it."

"I will. I promise."

By now, Dad was back. We helped him load up the small wooden cart, then followed him as he wheeled it over to the baggage clerk. For a few seconds, the sound of the liner's shrill whistle drowned out all the other noises on the pier. "That means you'd better get aboard," Dad said.

"Can I go with her?" I asked. "Oh, please, can I?"

Dad shook his head. "They're going to order the visitors off the ship anytime now."

I put my arms around Ellen and my tears dripped onto her jacket. "It's going to be awful here without you," I sobbed.

"Same here," Ellen sniffled. She gave me another hug, then pulled away and fumbled in her pocket for a hankie.

Dad gave Ellen's shoulder an awkward pat. "Like my wife said, we've been happy to have you stay with us. Come back anytime." In his patched overalls and faded work shirt—his hands roughened and calloused from years of hard work—he stood straight and tall, and I had a sudden glimpse of what he must have looked like when he and Mom had met, before his reddish-brown hair had thinned, before he had those tired lines around his eyes. It was an unexpected image, coming as it did at this particular moment.

Five minutes later the image was gone, because my full attention was focused upon Ellen as she walked up the gangplank, then turned to wave when she got to the crowded deck. How small she looked. If her jacket hadn't been such a bright red, I might have lost sight of her even before a group of passengers came between us. Then, even by squinting and straining my eyes, I couldn't see her anymore.

The ship's whistle blew its final mournful warning—the saddest sound I'd ever heard—and the gangplank swung away from the dock. It was final. Ellen was really leaving.

Dad and I stood there for a few moments. The ship's engines throbbed and a sea gull circled overhead. The air was ripe with the smell of fish and saltwater and rotting seaweed and creosote. Nearby stood a group of merchant marines, their seabags lying at their feet, cigarette smoke circling their heads.

* * *

One of the group, a bearded, broad-shouldered man, stepped toward me. "You look troubled, miss," he said, his deep voice filled with concern. "Can I be of help to you?"

I shook my head. "Thank you for asking, but no one can help me. I must cope with this loss by myself." Turning away, I strolled along the pier, listening to the restless water slap against the pilings, painfully aware of the emptiness in my heart.

Dad took my arm. "We have to go, honey," he said. The unusual gentle quality of his voice acted as a signal to the new round of tears I'd been holding back, and they spilled down my cheeks. Dad pulled out his big handkerchief from his back overall pocket and handed it to me as I blindly followed him to the car.

It wasn't until we were pulling away from the pier that I looked back at the ship, and a strange sensation crept over me. I felt as if I were caught in a sort of never-never land, a little island that stood between my past and my future. Somehow I knew that on this day—November 18, 1941—one chapter of my life had ended. I had no idea what the next chapter contained, but right now it didn't matter. I had no desire to turn the page.

Chapter 10

DAVE HAD NEVER SEEMED TO BE SENSITIVE TO MY EMOTIONAL ups and downs. Depending on his own particular mood, he teased me, or ignored me, or occasionally played the role of protector. During the first week after Ellen's departure, however, he was solicitous, almost deferential to me. I suppose he must have been aware of how much I missed Ellen, and on top of that, Prentice had received a ten-day leave and had gone to Minnesota to see his family. Ten days. An eternity. Whenever I thought about it, my stomach felt as if someone had punched me.

At first I appreciated Dave's thoughtfulness, but after a few days it made me feel as if there were a wall between us. I was relieved when he went back to calling me kid and rumpling my just-combed hair. On Thursday morning, exactly one week after Ellen had sailed, he threw a paper wad at me, making me spill the milk I was pouring over my cornflakes. Of course, Dad didn't see him misbehave. All he saw was me sopping up the milk with my napkin and sticking out my tongue at my pest of a brother.

"Mind your manners, young lady," he said, frowning at me over the rim of his coffee cup. I welcomed his grumpy look, because he, too, had seemed to be tiptoeing around my feelings.

Mom buttered a slice of toast. "Ellen ought to be just about getting to Honolulu by now," she said.

"Tomorrow. Probably just in time for Thanksgiving dinner." She's so lucky, I thought. Cruising over the blue Pacific. Will I ever make such a voyage? Maybe with Prentice . . . maybe . . .

We stood hand in hand, looking at the tropical moon in the cloudless sky. As the strains of a hauntingly beautiful melody floated from the ship's lounge, he took me in his arms. "This is just the first of many such memories," he murmured. "Together we shall travel to the four corners of the world, experiencing the best life has to offer."

"Tibet or Times Square," I replied, my voice husky with emotion. "It makes no difference as long as we are together."

"Marjorie, don't dawdle. You have to get to school." Mom's voice pulled me back into the dining room.

I shoved my chair back and picked up my cereal bowl and my Little Orphan Annie Ovaltine mug. "I'm going to be working with Kaye after school. Do you want me to pick up any last minute stuff for Thanksgiving dinner?"

Mom thought for a second, then shook her head. "No, I have everything."

Dave was ready to go about the same time I was, so we walked to the corner together. While we waited there for Larry, Dave kept giving me sideways looks and shifting from one foot to the other. "Something on your mind?" I asked, thinking that if he wanted to borrow some money, he was out of luck. I'd spent almost all of my allowance on a cream that was supposed to make my complexion smooth and radiant. Maybe it had been a waste of seventy-five cents, because after two days of following the instructions, after two days of squinting at the mirror, there was no sign of any of the "miraculous overnight results" the label had promised.

"No . . . well, yeah. You like this Prentice quite a bit, don't you?"

Now it was my turn to be nervous. If I said no, I'd be lying. But could I say yes? "What's it to you?" My face grew warm.

"It's just that . . . well, I'm a guy, and so is Prentice, and I know how he must feel, being so far away from home and all, and meeting a pretty girl."

Me? Pretty? Dave had never said anything like that to me before. Maybe that cream *was* working.

"I just want you to be careful. Don't let . . ."

"Hey—hi, Larry," I called, glad he showed up, because in spite of Dave's compliment, this conversation was making me feel uncomfortable.

And judging from the way the tenseness left Dave's expression, he was relieved, too.

With both Ellen and Prentice gone, Thanksgiving Day was just something to be endured. I was still feeling desolate when Larry dropped by early in the evening to help us eat up some of the leftovers. It was hard to feel sad when he was around, so by the time he left, the world was a lot less bleak. And then about seven o'clock, Prentice called me long distance!

"Just wanted to let you know I'm thinking about you," he said. "Hope you had a good day."

"Oh, sure," I said. "Except I wish that you had been here."

"Well, I'll be back in Dago on Sunday morning, so I can run up to see you for a few hours before I have to be back on base."

"Great. I'll save you some turkey, so you can have a sandwich."

By the time we said good-bye, I felt as if the sun had come out after a long, dreary winter.

Friday was spent reading and doing homework, then on Saturday Kaye and I got together to put the finishing touches on our lit project. As she read the final version aloud—as each carefully selected word, each painfully constructed phrase, combined to bring our ideas to life—I felt that my vague dream of becoming a writer was not such an impossible goal after all. Then, during the brief silence that followed Kaye's reading of the final sentence, I realized that as we had worked together on this project, we had done more than construct a fine bit of prose; we had shared a creative experience that went beyond anything that Ellen and I had ever shared. As I said good-bye to Kaye and walked up the hill toward home, this realization disturbed me. Ellen was, after all, my best friend.

Any distress I felt about my possible breach of friendship with Ellen was gone by Sunday morning. From the instant I opened my eyes, the refrain ran through my head—Prentice is coming! Prentice is coming! Even the weather seemed to be celebrating the event—although it had rained all night, the sun's rays were now making miniature rainbows in the droplets of water on my windowsill. And what made it even better was that Mom herself had suggested that I invite Prentice for lunch. I hadn't said much about his not being able to be with us on Thanksgiving, but she must have sensed how much I'd missed him.

It seemed that the morning would never pass, but finally the clock read 12:30 and I started combing out my pin curls, dabbling with the idea of sneaking into Mom's dresser drawer to use some of her lipstick. I quickly discarded the thought, not because it was wrong, but because Dad would be sure to notice and he wouldn't hesitate to send me out of the room to wipe it off even if Prentice was sitting right there to witness my humiliation.

Mom tapped on my bedroom door, then opened it and came in. "Anything I can do? Want me to help fix your hair?"

"Sure." I handed her my rat-tail comb. "I was sort of hoping to have a pompadour, then some curls right on the end."

"I'll try. Let's get some of this frizz out first." She picked up my brush. For the first few seconds she was quiet, then she said, "You really like Prentice, don't you?"

I nodded and began to blush, hoping she wouldn't get onto the subject that Dave had tried to talk about the other day.

"Your father and I always thought your first boyfriend would be someone from school. That way we'd be able to meet his family and get to know him. But a serviceman, well, he comes and goes, although I will say that Prentice seems very nice . . . so respectful and polite."

What a perfect opening. Now was the time to ask her the question I'd been wanting to ask all week. "He's always like that . . . it wasn't just a show to make you like him." I picked up a bobby pin, opened it, let it snap back, opened it again. "I've been hoping that now that you've met him . . . well, do you think there's any chance that you'll let me keep meeting him at the Skating Palace? I mean, even now that Ellen won't be there, too, and it'll be almost like having a date; he might get shipped out and we'll never get another chance and . . ."

I could see by Mom's image in the mirror that she was frowning. "That's exactly what your father and I are concerned about. Prentice won't be around long enough for you to get really acquainted, and with a serviceman there's always that pressure . . . the pressure to do things you shouldn't, because he might not be here next month, or even tomorrow." She laid the brush on the dresser and lowered her voice. "It's not that we don't trust you, dear. It's just that . . ."

The words trailed off, but the implication was as clear as as if she'd spelled it right out. She *didn't* trust me, and neither did Dave. Resentment flared up inside me, burning like a small angry flame. How dare they think that I would consider—or that Prentice would suggest—why, I couldn't even visualize the words that would describe the unthinkable act. Did my own family really believe I was like one of those girls at school who carry cigarettes in their purses and go to Tijuana on the weekends when even in my daydreams I never went beyond imagining how it would feel to have Prentice gaze into my eyes, then gently place his lips upon mine and hold me close and . . . ?

Mom's talk suddenly veered off in a different direction, jarring me, irritating me. "Maybe when you turn sixteen, you'll start going with someone from school. Someone you know—like Larry, for instance."

Larry! Of all the dumb ideas that took the prize. "Maybe," I said. Anything to end this little mother-daughter chat.

Mom smoothed down my hair and stood back. "Well, what do you think?"

"It looks great. Thanks a million." I was a little confused. While she had been warning me about becoming too involved with Prentice, she had been brushing and combing and fluffing my hair, making me look nice for the boy she was trying to discourage me from seeing.

After she had left the room, I went to my closet to pick out something to wear. Should it be my light blue skirt and fuzzy pink sweater, or my red dress with the flared skirt? Did I want to look soft and feminine, or vivid and provocative? What was the image of me that I wanted Prentice to carry until we were together again? I decided on the red dress, the one that Dave said reminded him of a fire engine. Thank goodness he had gone someplace with Larry for the afternoon.

And then Mom was calling me, telling me that Prentice had arrived, and I went into the front room to meet him. He smiled, and I could hardly breathe. How had I ever lived through the past week and a half? My fingers tingled in their eagerness to reach out to him.

"Take a load off your feet, young man," Dad said. He motioned for Prentice to sit on the couch, then he took a chair on the other side of the room. Holding my breath, feeling stiff and awkward, I walked between them and sat on the chair beside the telephone stand.

"So how are the marines treating you?" Dad asked. "Are you planning to make a career out of the service? You ever thought about going to college?"

"As a matter of fact, I have, sir," Prentice said. "But I decided that right now, with the draft and all, I'd better join up. After my hitch is over, I think I'll go to an agricultural college."

"Never knew you needed a degree to grow wheat and corn." Dad laughed, and I gritted my teeth, hating his attempt at humor, hating him for making Prentice the target of that humor.

But if Prentice was upset, he didn't show it. He just chuckled and said, "You don't, but what I want to do is work in the county farm bureau as an inspector or an advisor. I'll need a degree for that."

One by one, Prentice answered Dad's questions and remarks. Little by little, Dad's tone become less critical, less challenging. I leaned back in the chair, feeling the tenseness leave me. Oh,

Prentice, I'm so proud of you. Dad likes you. He even seems to respect you. It's going to be all right. It really is going to be fine.

By the time Mom brought in a plateful of turkey sandwiches and a bowl of potato salad, I had relaxed enough to hold up my end of the conversation that floated around the table. I even told one of my latest jokes—a really bad one—but Prentice and Mom laughed and I thought I saw a little smile pass over Dad's lips.

Mom had made sugar cookies for dessert. When Dad saw them, he reached into his pocket. "What are cookies without ice cream?" he said, handing fifty cents to Prentice. "Why don't you two stroll on up to the Orchid and get a pint of vanilla."

I held back a gasp. In my wildest dreams, I'd never imagined this would happen. Why, the Orchid was almost two miles away. If we went slowly, we'd have over an hour to hold hands, to talk, to . . .

Prentice shook his head, and my heart almost stopped. Didn't he want to be alone with me? "Please, let this be my treat," he said, and my heart started up again. A few minutes later, Prentice and I were walking up the hill toward Washington Street.

"Your folks are great," he said.

"I'm glad you think so."

"And you're not so bad yourself."

"Really?" First Dave, now Prentice. The more compliments I received, the prettier I felt.

"Yes, really."

As we turned the corner onto Washington, he took my hand and electric sparks chased up and down my arm. A few blocks farther on, the sidewalk ended, and we were walking along a dirt path that was bordered on one side by the curb, on the other by a small grove of peppertrees that were interspersed with honey-suckle bushes. As the slanting rays of the sun filtered through the rustling leaves of the overgrown trees, small shadows danced on the ground.

"There's Grant School," I said, pointing to the complex of cream-colored stucco buildings across the street. "That's where I went to grammar school."

Prentice didn't answer. Instead, he led me off the path, away from the street and out of sight of the occasional passing car. For the next few seconds, I was aware of nothing except the touch of his lips upon mine and the pinpoints of light that were flashing off and on in my head and the warm, melting sensation in my stomach and the scent of honeysuckle.

As we walked back out onto the path, scrunching fallen twigs and leaves beneath our feet, I felt giddy, glowing, a step away from reality. "Sorry." Prentice's eyes avoided mine. "I shouldn't have done that."

"No, no. It's all right." My voice sounded hoarse, the words forced, as my mind shouted, I *wanted* you to kiss me—I've been aching for it. I want you to hold me, to . . .

I choked back the unbidden thought, shocked at the realization that it had entered my mind. Was this what Mom and Dave had tried to warn me about? Was I one of *those* girls?

No, no, of course not. There's nothing wrong with kissing. That's what people do when they're in love. And Prentice and I are in love. In *love*! I was suddenly aware that everything I'd ever done in my life, every step I'd taken, every decision I'd made, had led me to this moment. And now that fate had brought us together, nothing would ever tear us apart.

Chapter 11

THE SUN SLIPPED BEHIND A CLOUD AND A LIGHT BREEZE RUS-
tled the leaves of the trees, but for me the world was standing still. I was
aware of nothing but the touch of his lips upon mine.

The kiss lasted but a moment, and as we continued our stroll, neither
of us spoke. Words, we knew, might break the spell . . .

It was the Thursday after Thanksgiving—exactly two weeks
since Ellen had left—and as I came home after school, I was reliving
that magical moment, trying to recapture the fleeting sensations
that had flooded over and through me, changing me forever. When
I reached the top of the hill, I turned and looked down on the
marine base, then, with a sigh, I walked slowly toward my house,
reluctant to release the memory and return to my family's colorless,
predictable little world—a world to which I no longer belonged.

I went up the back steps, hoping to walk through the kitchen
and into my room without being noticed. But there was Mom
coming out from her sewing room, a grin on her face, a mischievous
glint in her eyes. "Look on your desk," she said. "There's a nice
surprise waiting for you."

"A letter! It has to be a letter!" And sure enough there it was,
propped up against the lamp, an airmail envelope with Ellen's

slanty handwriting sprawled across its front. Throwing my books and purse on the bed, I picked it up, read the return address— 3160 Pahoa, Honolulu, Territory of Hawaii. Pahoa—what a lovely, musical, Hawaiian sound. After tearing open the envelope, I sat down and started to read. The letter was dated November 26.

Dearest Marjorie,

I haven't even finished my unpacking yet, but I just have to write to you. The trip was great. I didn't get seasick—Dad says I'm a born sailor. In the next-door cabin there was a woman about the same age as Mom, and she knew all about traveling on a ship, so I followed her around for the first couple of days. Then on the morning we docked, I met a girl who went to Hoover High! Can you believe it? She's really nice—not at all stuck-up like most of those Hooverites are. Her dad's in the navy, too.

One of these Sundays real soon, Dad says we can have breakfast in the ship's mess. Don't you envy me? All those sailors!! But of course, Mom and Dad will be there, so I won't have much of a chance to flirt. Not that I'd want to, of course. I miss Jack so much, and I haven't heard from him yet. Isn't that awful?

How are you and Prentice doing anyway? Has your dad let you keep on seeing him? I sure hope so.

Gotta run now. Please, please answer soon.

Lotsa love,
Ellen

I read the letter again to make sure I hadn't missed anything, then reached for a piece of notebook paper and wrote the date on the top—December 4, 1941.

Dearest Ellen,

I could hardly wait to hear from you and get your address, because I have something really great to tell you. Prentice kissed me! And I mean a real kiss, right on the lips. Did Jack ever kiss you? That's probably a dumb question, huh?

Have you started school yet? How's the weather there? Terrific, I bet. Have you eaten any poi? Does it really taste like paste?

Thanksgiving vacation was really quiet around here, except for Sunday, because that's when IT happened, right across from Grant School.

Answer right away. I MISS YOU!

Love,
Marjorie

P.S. Don't you dare let your mother see this letter. Burn it or tear it into little pieces.

Love,
Marj

I read what I had written, realizing that the words seemed to trivialize what had been, up to this moment, the most important event of my life. But could mere language describe what I had felt and what that kiss had meant to me? Perhaps it was better to keep my love for Prentice hidden in my heart, where it could grow and become strong enough to withstand exposure and the scrutiny of the outside world.

On the other hand, if I didn't share my secret with *someone*, I'd probably burst from the joy of it.

Prentice called me that night, even though he had to wait in line almost forty-five minutes to use the telephone. And he called me on Friday night to let me know he couldn't get a pass for Saturday, but he'd see me on Sunday. When the phone rang at 8:45 on Saturday night, I rushed to take the call, knowing it would be him, praying that nothing had happened that would prevent him from getting a pass. "Just wanted to let you know everything's on for tomorrow," he said. "I'll be leaving the base about noon."

"I'll be waiting," I said. "Maybe we can go for another walk." Another walk. Another kiss. My heart pounded as I put the receiver gently in the hook, mouthing the words, "I love you."

"That was Prentice," I said to Mom. "He'll be here tomorrow."

"Good," Mom said. "He can join us for an early supper." She had never again mentioned the reservations she and Dad had about my seeing a serviceman, but I sensed that they were on her mind every time Prentice's name was mentioned. Her occasional probing looks, her slight frowns, the quick glances that she and Dad exchanged at dinner—I knew that I was probably the subject of more than a few of their private conversations. I resented the fact that they were probably looking forward to the day that I had come to dread—the day when Prentice would be shipped out. It was just one more of the several things that were alienating me from the people who had always been closest to me.

None of this was enough to dampen my spirits as I washed my hair, rinsed it twice with vinegar to make it shine, then put it up in pin curls and went to bed, hoping to fall asleep right away so the night would pass more quickly. But sleep didn't come for over an hour. While raindrops pattered on the window, I lay first on one side, then on the other, then on my stomach, my head full of muddled thoughts of Ellen's letter, of Kaye, mostly of Prentice—and Prentice's lips on mine—and then all the thoughts blurred into each other and I was asleep.

The next morning I woke at nine, immediately aware that in three more hours Prentice would be walking out of the gates of the marine base. What a delicious, perfect afternoon it was going to be, but first I had to get through the morning. Somehow I ate my waffle, passed the syrup when Dad asked for it, and spoke when I was spoken to, while all I could think about was escaping from this ordinary routine into Prentice's embrace.

Two more hours. How slowly the hands of the clock moved as I cleared the table and filled the kitchen sink with hot water. And then the telephone rang and my heart stopped. *It's Prentice,* I thought. *He's going to tell me he can't come.* But it was just Larry calling Dave about a basketball practice, and my heart resumed its beating.

One more hour. Certainly if Prentice's pass had been canceled, he would have called by now. I went into my room, shut the door, and tried to read, but memories of that kiss came between me and the pages. Now it was eleven-forty. Time to decide what to wear and to comb out my pin curls. I turned on the radio and heard the trumpet of Harry James, my all-time favorite band-leader.

Suddenly the music was replaced with the voice of a newscaster and I started to switch stations. But something—perhaps the bleakness, the harshness, the urgency in that voice—stayed my hand, focused my attention on his words, words that I'd heard often enough as the German war machine had rolled across Europe and as Edward R. Murrow had described the air attacks on London. Injuries, deaths, confusion, panic, fire, terror.

But the newscaster wasn't talking about Paris or Leningrad. I leaned toward the radio, telling myself that I must have misunderstood.

"I repeat, the Japanese have bombed Pearl Harbor. The attack took our naval and air forces completely by surprise. . . ."

Pearl Harbor! Hawaii! No, no, it can't be . . . they wouldn't do that . . . not *us* . . . we aren't in the war . . . we . . . My mind could go no further. I stumbled toward the door.

As I entered the dining room, the only sound was the disjointed barrage of words coming from the Philco. Mom and Dad were standing motionless by the kitchen door. Dave was leaning over the radio, his face the color of ashes. The only touch of reality in the tableau was the aroma of fried bacon that lingered in the air.

"Casualties mounting . . . flames . . . shock . . . panic . . . *Kurusu* . . . no comment . . . complete surprise . . . Roosevelt . . . six battleships . . . the *Arizona* down . . ."

The *Arizona*! The name leaped out from all of the jumbled words and phrases that continued to pour from the speaker. Should it mean something special to me? For the moment, my mind refused to answer, so the fuzzy little question was tucked in among the avalanche of facts and figures and descriptions of this thing that I still couldn't believe was happening. Couldn't this be like the Orson Welles radio program a few years ago? The one in which he'd had everyone believing that Earth had been invaded by Martians and it had turned out to be nothing but an elaborate joke?

But, no. Somehow I knew this was no joke. This was undeniably, horrifying real.

I had no idea how long I stood there. Other commentators and government officials came on the air to express their outrage at what everyone called a "dastardly act, committed even as the Japanese envoys in Washington were talking peace." Finally, Mom walked over to me and put her arms around me. I started to tremble, but it was as if someone else was trembling.

"Ellen." That was all I could say.

"Shush," Mom said. "She's all right. I'm sure of it."

I was on the verge of believing her, but that elusive little detail that I'd been unable to pinpoint a few seconds ago suddenly shouted at me like a headline in a newspaper. "The *Arizona*! That's the ship Ellen's dad . . . Ellen was going to have breakfast there . . . some weekend soon, she said. What if it was today? What if . . . ?"

Mom gently covered my mouth with her hand. "Stop talking like that. You have to believe she's all right."

I looked up to see Dad standing by the window overlooking the bay, his thinning hair outlined above his head. "Well, this is it," he said. "I never thought it would happen, but this is war." He smacked his fist into the palm of his other hand as he turned to face us. "Damn. Too young for the last one and too old for this one."

"And you don't know how glad I am." Mom spoke so softly I doubted that Dad heard her.

"Are the recruiting offices open today?"

Dave had barely finished asking the question when Dad replied. "You are *not* going to enlist."

"But we'll have those Japs licked in no time. I want to get in on some of the action."

"The subject is closed, war or no war." Dad looked at Mom. "I'm going to give my notice at Spreckles and go to work at Consolidated. The sooner we get those planes built, the sooner we'll show those yellow devils who they've tangled with."

Dave stomped into his room. I started to follow him, to tell him I understood how he felt, to let him know I thought Dad was being unfair. Maybe Prentice could help. He could talk to Dad, convince him to . . .

Prentice. Oh, no. "All military leaves canceled," one of the newscasters had said. Where is Prentice right now? Will I be able to talk to him again—to say good-bye—to tell him I love him —that I'll wait for him?

Oh, please, please, let me hear his voice just one more time. There are so many things we've left unsaid. Don't let it be over. It barely had time to start!

Chapter 12

I WENT TO SLEEP THAT NIGHT PRAYING THAT PRENTICE WOULD call just one more time. *Just one more time.* Was that too much to ask? I woke up the next day, knowing that my prayer wasn't going to be answered. He was gone—vanished—as if the last few weeks had been nothing but a dream.

Somehow I got dressed, ate a slice of toast, and rode the bus and streetcar to school. As I put one foot ahead of the other, I felt as if I were slogging through mud. Why am I doing this anyway? I wondered. What's the use of studying about sixteenth-century England when Prentice is gone, and Ellen might be—might be . . . ?

I looked around me as I walked down the hall to my first-period class, listened to the kids laughing and talking, acting as if they hadn't heard about the awful thing that had happened.

But then three girls passed me, their faces grave. ". . . so awful," one of them said. "My brother is there. We're so worried about . . ." And then they were out of earshot.

"The Philippines, too," a boy was saying as he opened his locker. His friend shook his head, looking as if he didn't quite believe it.

Outside the attendance office a couple of teachers were looking at the front page of the *San Diego Sun*. PEARL HARBOR ATTACKED!

blared the big black headline. The teachers' faces were grim, their lips compressed. These adults, who had always seemed to have all the answers to everything, looked as helpless as I felt.

In my first-period math class, Mr. Hansen hurried through roll call, then immediately plunged into the lesson. "Turn to page sixty-six," he said. "Tom, go to the board and do the first problem." Stop it! I wanted to scream. Tell me why this thing has happened—tell me how you feel—are you angry?—are you frightened? . . .

But he said nothing about the bombing, the horrendous event that had disordered all our lives. He appeared, instead, to take refuge within his orderly little world of fractions and equations. At the end of the period he gave us our homework assignments, took off his horn-rimmed glasses, tucked them into his shirt pocket, and started wiping off the blackboard. But as I walked out the door, one of the last to leave the room, I glanced over my shoulder to see the board only half-erased and Mr. Hansen staring out the window, shoulders slumped, looking very alone.

In second-period American history, Miss Colbert marked her attendance sheet slowly and deliberately, her lined face pale under its light dusting of powder. When she closed her notebook, I reached for my pencil, ready to take notes, but she didn't say anything, just sat behind her desk, looking first at one pupil, then another. I glanced at the girl who sat across the aisle from me. Our eyes met. She shrugged.

When Miss Colbert finally spoke, her voice was soft, not dry and crisp as it usually was. "All of you know what happened yesterday," she said. "You realize, of course, that we must respond to the Japanese attack with a declaration of war. This will be an event of the greatest significance, not only in the history of our country, but in each one of our lives."

She cleared her throat and smoothed back her wispy gray hair, her hand trembling. "You're going to find great changes occurring, changes that you may not like or understand, but that will be necessary as we struggle to preserve our way of life.

"You are young, but you'll have opportunities to help in this struggle. I am not so young, but I'm going to do everything within my power to support our fighting men. Boys and girls, over the next few months, you're going to find . . ." Her voice broke. She covered her eyes and bowed her head. When she looked at us again, there were tears running down her wrinkled cheeks. "You're going to realize how precious, how unique our country is."

She reached for her purse, pulled out a lace-bordered hankie, and wiped her eyes. When she spoke again, her voice was steady. "Now open your books. Only by studying the past can we truly understand the present."

Tears blurred my vision. Never had a teacher moved me as Miss Colbert had with those few heartfelt words. I vowed never again to take my heritage, my country, for granted.

Miss Colbert had not only made me proud to be an American citizen, she had inspired me to do my part in defeating the enemy. Instead of sitting on the sidelines worrying about Ellen, longing for news of Prentice, I would sell defense stamps, collect pots and pans and toothpaste tubes and bacon grease, encourage others to do the same.

As if fate approved of my plans, during lunch Larry told me that he was forming a civil defense group and that the first meeting would take place that afternoon in Room 114.

"A lot of kids are interested," he said. "Invite anyone you think might want to help out."

At my request, each of the teachers in my afternoon classes made an announcement about the meeting. At 3:15, when I arrived, the large room was already half-full; one by one and two by two, more kids kept coming in. I waved at Dave, who was standing at one end of the front row, then took a seat near the rear door. A minute later, a girl sat down near me. I'd seen her in the lunch pergola a few times in the past couple of weeks, sitting alone, evidently a newcomer to San Diego High. She always ate quickly, her eyes downcast or buried in a book, not inviting any conversation. I knew it must have taken a lot of courage for her to come to this meeting by herself.

She brushed her stringy blond hair back from her face, pushed her wire-framed glasses up on her nose, and riffled through her notebook before pulling out a blank piece of paper—busy little activities perhaps calculated to cover up her nervousness.

"Hi," I said.

She turned her head with a quick, birdlike movement, a question in her eyes.

"I've seen you around," I added. "I'm Marjorie Ellison."

"I'm Doris Altman." Her slight smile flitted off and on. "I've seen you, too." When Larry stood up in front of the room and called for attention, she turned to face him, apparently dismissing my attempt at friendship.

"All right, listen up, everyone." Larry waited until everyone had stopped talking and rustling papers. "You all know why we're here . . . after what happened yesterday, we have a lot to do. For instance, what if we had a real emergency here in San Diego? Would we be able to handle it? How many of you know even the basics of first aid?"

Several kids raised their hands. "Well, that's a start," Larry said. "I've already asked Coach Riddle to spend some time with us going over the pressure points and how to treat burns and stuff. Now, we're going to need a telephone committee so we can keep in touch with each other. Who wants to do that?"

Doris started to put up her hand, pulled it down, then raised it all the way up.

Larry surveyed the room. "About twelve . . . great. Something else we have to get started on is learning to identify enemy planes. I'm going to get some of those cards . . . you know, the ones that have the silhouettes of different kinds of planes on them. We'll study them so we can tell our aircraft from the ones that belong to the Japanese."

Now, *that* was something useful and heroic! I'd seen women aircraft spotters in the war movies about London—they wore uniforms and kept watch while other citizens slept. I waved my hand in the air. "That's what I want to be . . . an aircraft spotter!"

A girl sitting in the front row giggled, and a couple of boys turned around to look at me, big grins on their faces. When someone else laughed, I squirmed, tempted to slide under the seat to get out of sight. Then Doris leaned toward me and whispered, "Good for you. Don't pay any attention to them."

"Hey, you'd be a good one, Marjorie," Larry said. "I'll let you know when I get the cards. Now, what about . . . ?"

My gratitude toward Larry and Doris was diluted by a rising swell of indignation. Let those know-it-alls laugh now, I thought. Just give me a chance—give me a really important job—and I'll show them how well I can handle it.

The night air was chill as I patrolled my assigned stretch of shoreline. My body was tense, my mind alert, as my ears strained in their attempt to pierce the thick fog that shrouded the city. My post was a crucial one, and I couldn't use the lack of visibility as an excuse for not spotting the outline of an enemy submarine rising from the depths of the sea.

Ah! The moon broke through the cloud cover, and there it was—an ominous black shape making its stealthy way toward the shore. With numbed fingers I pushed the button on my walkie-talkie. "Ellison reporting. Possible enemy sub sighted off the point."

"A naval unit is being dispatched," said a deep masculine voice. "Good work, Ellison. Because of you, the citizens of San Diego can . . ."

"Aircraft identification, first aid, collecting salvage, selling defense stamps and bonds . . . all that should keep us busy for a while," Larry was saying as my daydream clicked off. "I'd like to meet again next week at this same time. Those of you who have volunteered for the telephone committee give Dave here your names and telephone numbers. I'll take the names of the ones who want to take first aid training and collect salvage."

As a stream of kids flowed to the front of the room, Doris stood up, moved toward the aisle, then paused to look at me. "Marjorie? I just wanted to say . . . well . . ."

"What?"

"I think it was mean of those kids to laugh at you."

"Thanks, but I didn't mind. It was probably a pretty dumb thing to say anyway. Maybe I'd better settle for the telephone committee and salvage collection."

We walked down the aisle together and signed the sheet of paper that Dave handed us. When we were through, I introduced Doris to Dave. "Welcome to San Diego High," he said, turning to the next person who was waiting to sign up.

"Your brother's nice-looking," Doris said as we left the room.

"I suppose so. But he can be pesky sometimes. If you have a brother, you know what I mean."

"I don't have a brother." Doris paused. "And no sister either."

"Where do you live?" I asked.

"North Park."

"That's where my best friend used to live! But she's in Honolulu now." Please, Ellen, answer my letter. Tell me you're all right.

"My dad's in the army . . . in the Philippines. We were all packed up to go there . . . until yesterday."

"Oh, gosh, I bet you're worried."

Doris was silent, her face expressionless.

"Want to eat lunch together tomorrow?" I asked.

"Sure. In the pergola?"

"Right."

By now we were passing the open doors of the auditorium where the school chorus was singing "O Little Town of Bethlehem." I glanced at Doris, wondering how she felt as she listened to the sounds of Christmas.

Christmas! My gosh, how can *anyone* think of celebrating the holidays this year? Not Prentice. Not Ellen, even if she's all right. Certainly not me. Who can think of stringing colored lights on a tree or basting a turkey now that we've been attacked? Now that Prentice is gone—now that Ellen might be—might be . . .

Stop it. Don't think about that word. To do so makes the possibility much too real, brings the war much too close.

Chapter 13

WE'RE AT WAR—REALLY AT WAR. THE WORDS ECHOED IN MY head as we sat around the dinner table listening to the speech President Roosevelt was making to Congress.

"Yesterday, December seventh, nineteen forty-one—a date which will live in infamy—the United States of America was suddenly and deliberately attacked by naval and air forces of the empire of Japan. The United States was at peace with that nation . . . and was still in conversation with its government and its emperor, looking toward the maintenance of peace in the Pacific . . ."

None of us was touching the food on our plates. We all strained forward to hear each measured phrase. ". . . With confidence in our armed forces, with the unbounded determination of our people, we will gain the inevitable triumph, so help us God."

The president paused. My muscles tensed, preparing for the words I knew were coming.

"I ask that the Congress declare that since the unprovoked and dastardly attack by Japan on Sunday, December seventh, nineteen forty-one, a state of war has existed between the United States and the Japanese empire."

I didn't move. I barely breathed, and yet my muscles involuntarily relaxed after hearing, with my own ears, the declaration of war. Dad turned down the volume on the radio. "So that's it," he said, his tone of voice reflecting a sad resignation to our forced entry into the battle. "And you can bet your bottom dollar that the next step will be a declaration against Germany and Italy, too." He shook his head. "A two-front war. Are we up to it?"

Mom picked up her fork, held it in midair, then put it back on her plate. "John, I'm going to go to work." She spoke matter-of-factly, and the determined set of her chin told me that, if necessary, she was prepared to fend off a barrage of objections.

"You work?" Dad shook his head. "Don't be silly. You have no experience. Besides, there's more than enough to keep you busy right here at home." He picked up his newspaper, a signal that the discussion was over.

"John, listen to me," Mom persisted. "I mean it . . . I'm going to get a job. The papers says Consolidated needs workers, experienced or inexperienced."

Dave and I exchanged furtive glances as we waited for Dad's expression of outrage at this act of rebellion. But he said nothing, just looked at us, then at Mom.

"I want to help," Mom said. "I can't just stand by and . . ."

"We'll discuss this later." Dad's voice was restrained. "When we're alone." He hid his wounded pride behind the open newspaper.

Mom attacked her portion of pot roast with her knife and fork. This was not the meek-mannered, eager-to-please woman that Dad had grown accustomed to. We had been at war for only a few hours, and it looked as if it was war at home, too.

The shrill ringing of the telephone ended the silence that had settled over the table. I jumped up to answer it.

"Marjorie? Kaye. I just got a terrific idea for our paper. Can you come down for a few minutes?"

I hesitated. If Dad had been against my associating with the Narasakis before the bombing, he certainly would be even more so now. Besides, he'd just been challenged by Mom, right in front of Dave and me, and was not likely to be in the mood to say yes to anything. "Gee, I don't know . . . can't we do it over the phone?"

"It would be hard. I promise it won't take long at all." There was a note of insistence in her voice, a hint that she had more on her mind than a revision of our paper.

Anticipating Dad's explosive vocal reaction, I covered the mouthpiece with the palm of my hand. "Dad? It's Kaye. She wants to see me . . . it's about our lit project." Gritting my teeth, I braced myself for his indignant outburst.

His face turned brick red as he slammed his coffee cup down on his saucer. "Are you crazy, girl? I forbid it."

My own indignation gave me courage. "But all I want to do is finish up my paper. It's important. Please?" I glanced at Mom, pleading silently for support.

"John, for heaven's sake, let her go," Mom said. "It is for school, after all."

Dad pushed his plate aside, although his dinner was only half eaten. "Do what you damn well please. Evidently what I want means nothing in this family." He stood up, strode across the room and onto the front porch, slamming the door behind him.

Mom started piling up the dishes. "Go ahead," she said. "He'll be all right."

After telling Kaye I'd be right down, I hung up the phone and gave Mom a quick kiss on her cheek. "Thanks. I won't be gone long." To avoid confronting Dad, I took the back stairs.

As I walked down the hill, I felt no satisfaction in my small triumph over Dad's authority; I felt, instead, a persistent nudge from my conscience. It wasn't just that I didn't like to see my father put in an awkward position; it was that I was beginning to wonder if he may have been right about my associating with the Narasakis. I found it hard to admit, even to myself, but sometime during the last couple of days, little shadows of uncertainty had begun to cloud my attitude toward my Japanese friends. Not that I thought they were spies, and I was sure they hadn't been involved in the bombing. But wasn't it possible that they *knew* someone who had helped to plan or carry out the sneak attack? Maybe a cousin or a friend—one of those people from whom Mr. Narasaki received letters. If that were true, then when push came to shove, whose side would they be on?

Those vague shadows hovered over me as I walked into the store and stood face-to-face with Kaye and her parents. "Hi," I said, taking my hands out of my jacket pockets, then putting them back in, shifting my weight back and forth from one foot to the other.

"Hi." Kaye's beautiful dark eyes contained an unspoken question, and I was now certain that she was wondering whether or not our friendship had become a casualty of the attack on Pearl Harbor. I wanted to remove her doubts, to assure her that nothing had changed between us, but I couldn't, because things *had* changed, no matter how much I wished otherwise. For a brief moment I resented the fact that she had knowingly placed me in this uncomfortable situation.

Mr. Narasaki half smiled and nodded at me, then continued to sort out the receipts that were spread out on the counter. Mrs. Narasaki said hello, very formally, very politely, then busied herself with straightening some shelved cans, although those cans were already lined up in pinpoint precision.

"Come on upstairs," Kaye said.

"Right." I followed her up the narrow flight of steps that led to their living quarters above the store. Their apartment contained two bedrooms that were actually only curtained alcoves, a tiny kitchen, and a living area where Paul slept when he was home. His rollaway bed was standing at the head of the stairs.

"See Paul's picture by the telephone?" Kaye gathered up some typed pages. "It was taken right after his basic training."

I walked to the other side of the room to get a closer look at the photograph. Paul's eyes, under his visored army hat, were filled with intelligence and gentleness. "He looks really good in a uniform," I said. "More handsome than ever."

"Sit down," Kaye said, motioning to a wooden kitchen chair that stood beside the oilcloth-covered kitchen table. In the center of the table was a bouquet of pansies arranged in a dainty flat bowl. At the sight of those purple flowers, my tension started to dissolve. The Narasakis were good people, and Kaye was still Kaye, wasn't she? No matter what happened yesterday, no matter what would happen tomorrow.

"Now, here's what I was thinking," Kaye said. "On page ten, what if Hamlet told Ophelia . . . ?"

Forty minutes later, as we put our pencils down, I still wasn't sure about Kaye's purpose in having me come to see her. It was true the paper was improved, but I was sure we would have received an A even without the slight revisions.

"Good job," Kaye said, stretching her arms over her head. "We've no doubt made literary history."

"Sure. A hundred years from now some teacher will be telling some poor kids to memorize the immortal lines written by Ellison and Narasaki. Can't you just hear the groans?"

Kaye didn't laugh. I pushed my chair back, sensing what was

coming next and wanting to avoid it. "I went off and left the dishes. Guess I'd better get going."

"Wait . . . wait." Kaye frowned and shook her head. She seemed to be struggling to get her thoughts in order. "We have to get something straightened out. I know that . . . well, it was obvious you felt uneasy when you came into the store tonight." She lowered her gaze and paused for a moment. "Seems that a lot of people feel that way now, but that doesn't bother me . . . at least not too much." Now she was looking straight at me. "I do care about you, though . . . so do my parents . . . we want to keep on being friends . . . to . . . ."

Tears glistened on her eyelashes. I reached for her hand, suddenly aware that these words had to be said and glad that it was happening here instead of at school, where there would be inquiring eyes, accusing glances.

Now, however, it was my turn to grope for the right words, and it was difficult because memories had come flooding into my head. There were the times that Mrs. Narasaki had sent tea roses home to my mother; the way Paul used to wink at me as if we were sharing a special secret; Mr. Narasaki's infinite patience as he tried to teach me the Japanese language, his warm smile when I succeeded in understanding some tricky bit of grammar.

But then, smack in the middle of those memories, was a chilling black headline—PEARL HARBOR ATTACKED! All those people killed. Maybe Ellen. Soon, maybe Prentice. Part of me wanted to say the words that would erase the pain and uncertainty in Kaye's eyes. Another part of me wanted to admit that Dad was right after all. What was more important—my friendship with Kaye or my country?

My silence was telling Kaye more about my ambivalence than any speech could have. She stood up. "I understand." Her face was expressionless.

"No, you don't. I do want to be friends. It's just that . . ." For a moment I toyed with the idea of telling her how Dad felt, but discarded it when I realized that would only be an excuse for my own weakness and indecision.

"Don't explain. It's all right. I know things have changed." Kaye picked up the papers that were scattered on the table. "Our project is finished."

I could think of nothing to say as I followed her down the stairs. Mr. and Mrs. Narasaki said good-night, just as formally and politely as they had greeted me, and I said good-night back. As the door swung shut behind me, I was heavyhearted and perplexed and relieved all at the same time. But there was something else as well. Guilt? That's what it was. Instead of the reassurances that Kaye had been asking for, I had wounded her. Me, who yelled at Dave if he stepped on a spider, and became angry when someone struck a dog or a cat, had deliberately injured a friend.

Changing directions, I hurried back to the store. Through the window I saw Kaye wiping away tears as she talked to her parents. When I opened the door, the three of them turned to me, their expressions wary.

"I forgot to tell you I wrote to Paul, and a couple of days ago I got a postcard from him. See you at school, Kaye. Maybe we can ride home together."

"If you like," Kaye replied with a hesitant smile.

Mrs. Narasaki stepped forward to kiss my cheek. "Stop in to say hello. The water will be boiling for tea."

I left the store and walked toward the corner, passing a newspaper rack on the way. IT'S WAR! the headlines shouted. Such stark, cold, ugly words, but my cheek was still warm where Mrs. Narasaki's forgiving kiss had left its soft imprint.

Chapter 14

WAKE ISLAND OVERRUN! GUAM FALLS! PHILIPPINES UNDER siege! All during Christmas vacation the news reports and headlines brought us nothing but bad news. To me, though, the worst part was checking the mailbox twice every day and finding nothing but bills and advertisements and greeting cards from people we saw all the time or people we hadn't heard from since the end of last year. I had written to Ellen three times, begging her tell me that she was all right, but she hadn't answered. And there was nothing from Prentice either. Sometimes I felt like running after the mailman, begging him to look through his bag again. But, of course, I never did, because if he didn't find anything, I probably would have started crying right there in front of him.

Dad had gone to work at Consolidated, and since he had volunteered to work four hours on Christmas Day, we had to squeeze our dinner and the opening of our presents around his shift. While the turkey was roasting, Mom and I covered the windows with dark material, because all of San Diego had to be blacked out. As we attached the cloth to the big front-room window, Mom paused to look toward the downtown area. "The war's taken away my jewelry box," she murmured.

She was referring to the thousands of city lights that would no longer be sparkling like diamonds displayed on black velvet. Mom had always seemed to find comfort in the sight of those lights. It seemed to me that they represented her hope for a better life; they enabled her to accept the worn sofa and the threadbare carpeting that faced her when she turned away from the window. Now that she would no longer have her jewelry box, would her dreams also disappear?

I felt a surge of panic. Would the war make *my* dreams disappear? Prentice . . . Prentice . . . where are you? The decorated tree, the packages under it, the promise that Christmas had always brought with it—none of it held any meaning for me this year.

When vacation was over, I did the usual things—went to school, hung out the laundry, ran the carpet sweeper—but all around me things were changing. Anchored by their long cables, barrage balloons floated above the coastline. Consolidated Aircraft, which had always been a silvery color, was being painted a battleship gray and its roof covered with green netting. I supposed when the camouflage was finished, from an airplane the building would look like a field of alfalfa.

And there were soldiers everywhere. Every time I walked up or down Pringle Hill, at least four or five army trucks and jeeps passed by, the distinctive whining sound of their motors giving me warning so I could brace myself for the inevitable chorus of wolf whistles and hey, babes. And then a small antiaircraft unit set up camp in the vacant lot directly across the street from our house. There they were, all those uniformed men living almost in our front yard. One day I was sweeping the sidewalk and one of them—a freckle-faced private—crossed the street and stood on the curb a few feet away from me. "Jist wanted to tell y'all that us yardbirds are mighty pleased to have such a fine-lookin' filly passin' by every day."

Before I had a chance to say anything, he blushed and ran back across the street. I stood there motionless, propped up by the broom, as he disappeared into a tent. The other soldiers grinned and waved at me. It wasn't until that evening that I figured out what had happened—that poor, bashful private had been given a dare to come over and talk to me. But had he been told what to say, or had the compliment been his own idea? No matter—I made up my mind right then that never again would I go outside with my hair in pin curls.

Doris and I were eating lunch together every day and going to Larry's civil defense meetings a couple of times a week. One Friday afternoon we were standing on the streetcar landing in front of school. "Want to go to a movie tomorrow?" I asked.

She shook her head and gave me the same answer she always did. "Have to stay with Mom."

"How is she anyway?"

"Not good. Just sits there waiting to hear something about Daddy. The other day she started crying and I didn't think she'd ever stop."

"Wow, that must have been awful." I knew how she felt, because every time I opened the mailbox and there was nothing there for me, my heart tumbled from my chest into my stomach.

Kaye had come down the steps and joined a couple of other Japanese girls who were standing a few feet away from us. She grinned when she saw me looking at her. "Hey," she called. "Do you think all that work was worth it?"

Mrs. Gilmore had handed our term papers back that morning,

and on the top of ours there was a big A+ and the comment, "Good work!" "You know it," I called back. "Let's get together and have a soda to celebrate."

"Sure thing," Kaye said.

I turned back to Doris. "Mrs. Gilmore really liked—" I stopped, startled by the cold glint in her eyes and the stony set of her face. "What's wrong?"

"How can you talk to them?" Doris said. "After what they did . . . after . . ."

"But she's my friend. I've known her for ages."

"She's nothing but a sneaky Jap. You can't—"

"Stop it! Don't be crazy. Kaye doesn't have anything to do with what's happening. It's not her fault that your dad . . ."

Sparks filled Doris's usually placid eyes. "What do *you* know about it?" She spat the words at me. "*Your* father's here, safe and sound. You don't have any idea . . ."

By now, some kids who were standing close by were staring at us, but I didn't care. "I do so. My best friend might be—might be . . ." Even in the heat of anger I couldn't say that most final of all words.

"See you around," Doris said, and a moment later she was boarding her northbound streetcar. I stared after her, shaken by our bitter exchange, then jumped when I felt a light tap on my shoulder.

Whirling around, I saw Larry and Beverly Rhodes. "Hi," Larry said. "Bev here is going to come to our next meeting. Not only that, she's volunteered to bring some cookies and punch."

Beverly stepped forward, smiling, showing her perfect teeth. "Oatmeal and raisin," she said. "Larry says they're his favorite."

"Great." Just in time the number twelve streetcar rattled to a stop on the other side of the landing. "You going straight home, Larry? Want to ride together?"

"Might as well." He turned to Beverly. "Have a good weekend. I'll be calling you."

Pushed along by ten or fifteen other kids, Larry and I got on the streetcar and found a seat by the back window. Larry put a nickel in the gum machine that was attached to the wall and yanked the lever. Nothing came out. Two more yanks. Still nothing. "Oh, well," he said, settling back. "Guess I can get along without it."

"Hey, you just lost a nickel. You should be mad."

"Not worth it. When I get upset, it's got to be about something important."

"You're smart. When I think about how I used to grumble about Ellen using my hairbrush or taking up too much room in the closet . . . well, that was dumb . . ." I let my voice trail off, unwilling to reveal my hidden guilt. "Anyway, who needs gum when Beverly's baking her oatmeal cookies?" I gave him a sideways look. "Are they really your favorite?"

Larry grinned. "Come on, you know the answer to that one, but when she told me that was the only kind she knew how to make, what could I say?"

So I'd been right. It was peanut butter cookies that he liked, the ones my mom made, the ones he'd been eating at our house ever since he'd started coming around.

I had said so long to Larry and was walking up our front steps when I saw the mailman turn the corner. I waited, praying, as he tucked a couple of envelopes into Mrs. Morris's mailbox and started toward our house. Please. Please. My heart pounded. Now he was standing right in front of me, sorting through some letters. "Ah, here we are," he said. "Not too much this afternoon."

A telephone bill and something from Montgomery Ward. "That's all?"

" 'Fraid so. Have a nice evening." He strode off down the street, unaware that my world revolved around his twice-a-day visits.

Maybe something came in the morning mail, I thought. Don't count on it though. Don't even hope, because you'll only end up being disappointed again. Dave came out from his room when I walked into the house. Any mail? I wanted to ask, but didn't, because I couldn't bear to hear the answer.

"Hi," I said.

"Hi." He stood there as if he expected me to say something else.

"What's going on?" I asked.

Dave shrugged. "Nothing much."

"Oh." I started toward my room.

"By the way, you might be interested in this," Dave said.

I turned to see that he was holding an envelope. "A letter! You brat! Who's it from?" I ran to him and grabbed for it, but he held it above his head, just out of my reach. "Give it to me. I *hate* you!"

"Oh, all right. I give up." He handed it to me. "It's from some leatherneck . . . Prentice somebody-or-other. Nothing important."

Pfc. Prentice Moreland—that was the beautiful name in the upper left-hand corner. "Just you wait," I said to Dave. "You're going to pay for this." Actually, I felt like kissing him. I would have kissed *anyone* who had given me this letter.

I shut my bedroom door and took another look at the envelope. How strong and clear his handwriting was. My fingers were trembling so much I had trouble tearing open the flap, and the paper shook as I soaked up each beautiful, precious word.

"Dearest Marjorie," he had written. Dearest. He had said *dearest*.

You know I can't tell you where I am, but there's a (censored) and there are (censored). Sounds a lot like (censored), doesn't it? Whoops! I forgot how upset you get when I call your hometown by its nickname.

So far, there's not much going on here. Just a lot of scuttlebutt going around. I'm really sorry I didn't have a chance to say good-bye to you. Everything happened so fast. One minute we were in the rec hall playing Ping-Pong, the next we were on our way to (censored), and from there we were loaded onto a troop ship.

I think about you a lot and wish we could have had more time to get to know each other. Write when you can and don't skate with too many swabbies!

Love, Prentice

I read the letter two more times, reveling in every comma, every period, even the places that had been cut out by the censor, that unknown person who had seen this letter, who had dared to obliterate parts of Prentice's thoughts. But I forgave this stranger almost immediately. He was, after all, doing it for the sake of security, for Prentice's safety.

I folded the paper, reverently slipped it back into the envelope, feeling that I'd burst if I didn't share this news with someone. Not Dave. He'd make light of it. Mom? Where's Mom? When I asked Dave, he shrugged, shook his head, and turned his attention back to the *Collier's* magazine he was reading. Kaye? No, she'll be busy waiting on the afternoon rush of customers. Doris. That's it. I'll call Doris.

I dialed her number and waited, tapping my foot, listening to one ring, two rings, three rings. "Hello?" The voice sounded muffled, only vaguely familiar.

"Doris?"

"Yes."

"Hi, this is Marjorie. The best thing happened . . . I got a letter from Prentice. Can you believe it? This must be a dream. Tell me it's not a dream and that any minute I'll wake up and . . ."

I stopped to catch my breath, to give Doris a chance to say something, but there was no sound on the other end of the line.

"Doris? You're not still mad, are you? Please don't be mad."

"No, that's not it. I'm happy for you."

"You sound funny," I said. "What's the matter?"

"It's just that . . ." Again there was no sound until I heard what sounded like a sob. "Well, we got this telegram. It was about Daddy."

"He's not—he's not—"

"He's missing in action. Mom's taking it pretty hard."

"But missing just means they don't know, doesn't it? He could be all right." Words. Meaningless words, but I had to say something, didn't I?

"I keep saying that to Mom, but she just keeps crying and then I start crying and . . . oh, it's awful."

"If we can help . . ."

"Thanks, but there's nothing anyone can do."

"I'll call you tomorrow, okay?"

I put the receiver back on the hook. Missing in action. Killed in action. Every day hundreds of people were getting those telegrams, including Mr. Hansen—his only son had been killed during the Japanese invasion of Guam. I wanted to tell him how sorry I was, but he left no opening in the wall he seemed to have built around himself; the only signs of his grief were an occasional moment of distraction and his paler-than-usual complexion.

Picking up Prentice's letter, I looked at the date. January 14.

That's when he had written it. On that day he was alive and well, but that was two weeks ago. It doesn't tell me anything about how he is right now, right this minute, I thought. This war makes everything—even life itself—*especially* life itself—seem so—so *temporary*.

Just a few moments ago, I'd been ecstatic, eager to share my joy with anyone who would listen. And now? My instincts told me that this would spoil my good fortune, might even put Prentice in jeopardy. I traced my finger over his signature at the end of the letter, vowing to keep his words hidden in my heart, realizing that the uncertainty about his fate, the agony of not knowing, had started all over again.

Chapter 15

MY DARLING,

There are not enough words in the English language to tell you how much I miss you. Since you left, the days are endless and the nights . . . well, the moon's appearance serves only to remind me that you are not here to share the evening with me . . .

Saturday, February 14, 1942

Dearest Prentice,

It's raining today, but when your second letter came, it made me feel as if the sun was shining, so I'll answer it before I finish my homework. (Lots of math. Ugh!) The big news is that yesterday I got a letter from Ellen! I was glad to find out she's all right, but sad when I found out that her father had been on the Arizona *when it went down. I feel so awful when I think of what she must be going through.*

Mom's going to start work at Consolidated on Monday. In fact, she was down there applying on the afternoon I got your first letter. Don't ask me how she talked Dad into it.

> *Maybe the biggest piece of news is that right this min-*
> *ute Dave's downtown having his physical for the marines.*
> *I've been keeping my fingers crossed all day that he passes.*
> *(Now you know why my handwriting's so bad—ha!).*
> *Larry seems to have gotten over being rejected, but I don't*
> *think Dave could stand being a 4F.*
>
> *Oh, how I envy Dave, and you, too. If only I could do*
> *something to help win the war.*
>
> *Please write soon and often and take care of yourself.*
>
> > *Love,*
> > *Marjorie*

Before I slipped the letter into an envelope, I read it through again and realized how short it came of describing my real feelings, my dreams. But how could mere words describe the soaring of my heart when I thought of him, the warmth that flooded my being when I remembered his kiss? Was there any way I could make him aware of how I longed for his presence, a longing that was both bitter and sweet at the same time? How could I capture these feelings on paper so he could carry them in his heart as he faced the fury of the enemy?

To a lesser degree, I felt the same inadequacy when I tried to answer Ellen's letter. How could I make her understand my envy when she had sailed for Honolulu and I'd had to stay behind wishing that my father were in the navy, and now her father was dead and I was so relieved that my own father was alive—and how guilty I felt for allowing my confused emotions to prevent my sharing her grief and her pain—"Dearest Ellen," I finally wrote. "I'm so sorry about your father. Are you all right? How is your mother? Please let me know if I can do anything to help." I chewed on the end of my pencil for a moment, then added, "I think about you all the time. Love, Marjorie."

There was really nothing more I could say. I hoped that Ellen would be able to read between the lines and know that my heart ached along with hers and that I wanted her to forgive me for the times when I was impatient with her and that she'll know I really am her friend.

The house was quiet with Mom and Dad out shopping for groceries and Dave at the recruiting office. Too quiet. I felt a sudden need to get away from this room and the stillness that allowed me to dwell on my depression. Glancing at the clock on the dresser, I saw it was only 3:30. If I hurried I could get to the bottom of the hill and mail my letters in time to get collected in the last pickup. I tied a bandanna around my head, put on my raincoat and galoshes, and went outside. Donnie, the soldier who had taken his buddies' dare, was leaning against the telephone pole in front of the encampment, not seeming to mind the soggy weather at all. We waved at each other as I walked toward the corner.

"Good weather for ducks," he called.

"Quack, quack," I replied, and his laughter followed me as I started down the hill.

Although the rain was steady, there was no wind and I was warm inside my raincoat. When I was a little girl, this kind of weather invited me to wade in puddles and sail stick sailboats in the gutters. And when the rain let up, Dave and Larry and I had played mumblety-peg in the damp dirt or went across the street to the vacant lot to pull wild oats up by the roots and throw the muddy weeds at each other.

After I had dropped the letters in the box, I glanced at the Narasakis' place and was struck by how forlorn it looked. A couple of weeks ago, they'd hung a white banner across the front of their store. Its black letters spelled out WE ARE AMERICANS! and it had looked so proud and clean and brave as it flapped in the wind. Now those same letters were runny and blurred and the banner clung damply to the siding.

I stood there for several moments, wanting to go back home, wanting to forget that lonely looking little building, but feeling myself pulled toward it. Then, almost without getting a signal from my brain, my feet took the first steps toward the store, my hand opened the door, my ears heard the cheerful jingling of the bell that was attached to it.

Kaye was sweeping the floor, but she put the broom aside when she saw me. "Hi." Her smile tried to be bright and welcoming, but her eyes had lost some of their luster.

"Didn't have much to do, so I thought I'd drop in."

"Thanks. Not many people have been doing that lately." She shrugged. "But then, maybe it won't make too much difference anyway."

"Why?"

"We got a letter from the government saying it would be better if we moved away from the coast . . . for our own safety, it said, but we know what it meant. Mom and Dad want to try to stick it out though. They don't feel up to starting over somewhere else."

"I hope you can stay," I said. I couldn't imagine anyone else running this store. I'd never be able to look at it again.

"It's funny, isn't it?" Kaye's voice was bitter. "There are plenty of Italians and Germans around, but they get to stay where they are."

"It's not fair." I took off my bandanna, wadded it up, and put it in my pocket, wishing I could do something to make their situation better, feeling powerless. I looked away from her and concentrated on the raindrops running down the window. "Guess I better get home," I said after a few moments of strained silence. "Tell your folks hi for me."

"I will."

With my hand on the doorknob, I turned back to her. "They can't make you go away. It's not right."

Kaye smiled again. "That's what I keep telling myself. I'll see you at school tomorrow, okay?"

I stepped onto the rain-slicked sidewalk, again painfully aware of the impermanence that the war had brought. The Narasakis had lived here for almost twenty years; now they might be forced to move. The people around Five Points and as far away as Old Town had been their steady customers—some of them had been their friends—and now those same people were going to Piggly Wiggly or Safeway.

Maybe—the thought was painful—maybe the Narasakis *would* be better off someplace else. I'd seen with my own eyes how the Japanese kids were being treated at school. Just a couple of days ago, a senior—a big football-player type—had said some awful things to a Japanese boy who was only a tenth-grader and about half his size. "Sneaky little Nip." "Yellow devil." The epithets had been thrown like daggers, but their target didn't flinch, just turned and walked down the hall, his back stiff and proud, looking straight ahead. What courage that must have taken.

The rain had brought back a lot of happy memories as I'd been walking down the hill. Now it just made my world cold and sodden and gray.

I didn't have much time to see the Narasakis for the next couple of weeks, because Mom kept me so busy cleaning the house. Dave was leaving for boot camp—why in the world had he been assigned to Quantico, Virginia, instead of right here in San Diego?—and she wanted to see him off with a small dinner party just before he had to catch his train.

I figured Larry would be invited, but was really surprised to find that Doris was coming, too. She and Dave had been dating for a whole month and neither one of them had said a word about it to anyone! I didn't wonder why Dave hadn't. He never had been one for talking about his social life. But why had Doris been so closemouthed about it? It wasn't that she didn't have plenty of chances to say something—we saw each other at least two or three times a day at school and talked on the phone a lot.

At first, I felt hurt—after all, I had shared a lot of her unhappiness about her father. Shouldn't I have shared some of the good things in her life? But after I thought it over, I realized that I should have expected as much, because Doris had always been full of secrets. I'd told her my life history, but all I knew about her was that she'd traveled from army post to army post. I'd talked about how my dad bossed my mom around and how she had stood up to him and got a job, but Mrs. Altman remained a mystery woman, a shadowy figure who apparently spent her days waiting for further word about her husband.

And I had told her all about Prentice and how he had kissed me and what a good skater he was, but when it came to how she had been dating my own brother—well, she'd kept *that* to herself, like it was something to be ashamed of.

On the day of the dinner, Mom was up early making a lemon meringue pie—Dave's favorite—and baked ham with candied yams—also Dave's favorite. Dave and Dad sat in the living room for almost an hour without yelling at each other even once. In fact, while I was setting the table, I heard Dad say, "I'm proud of you, son. And I can't help envying you. Wish I were young enough to join up and show those devils a thing or two."

About one o'clock, there was a knock on the door and Dave jumped up to answer it. It was Doris, looking—well, not exactly pretty, but her hair was shiny and her eyes were bright and her cheeks had a glow to them, almost like she'd used rouge, but I knew it was because she was happy.

A short while later, Larry arrived. "Good to see you," Dad said to him. "You've been staying away too much."

"Been busy with school and stuff." Larry didn't sit down until Mom pushed a chair up for him. Then instead of settling back and tossing wisecracks around, he was strangely quiet. Of course, with Dave and Dad and even Doris laughing and talking so much, maybe he was having a hard time getting a word in edgewise. By this time Mom didn't need my help anymore, so I sat on the arm of Dad's big upholstered chair. "I sold my bike and used the money to buy war stamps," I said to Larry. "It was enough for almost two whole books."

"That's great."

"Did Dave tell you I finally heard from Ellen?"

"No. She's all right, then?"

"Yes, but . . ."

"All right, dinner's ready," Mom said. Everyone got up and I didn't get to finish telling him the bad news about Ellen's dad.

Later, as the ham and potatoes were being passed around for second helpings and we were all telling Mom how good everything tasted, Larry had relaxed a little. When Doris started telling us about her volunteer work at the naval hospital, he looked at me. "Hey, Marj, have you ever thought about being a bandage roller?"

The hospital was right next door to San Diego High, and every time I looked at it, I thought about all those sick and injured men. Maybe dying men. "Me work in a hospital? I don't think so . . . no, I couldn't."

"But it's not like what you think," Doris said. "I just talk to the guys and play checkers and Monopoly and stuff."

"It might be a good idea," Mom said, but the look on Dad's face told me he didn't agree. For once, I thought he was right.

"Mom, this ham's fantastic," Dave said. "I bet when I'm chowing down on that mess hall food, I'll be thinking how good all you civilians have it."

Larry had been reaching for one of Mom's homemade Parker House rolls, but he suddenly pulled his hand back. Wiping his mouth with his napkin, he stood up. "That really was good, Mrs. Ellison, but I'm afraid I'm going to have to eat and run. Lot of things going on this afternoon."

Dad raised his eyebrows in surprise. "Aren't you coming along to see Dave off?" he said. "We'll squeeze you into the car somehow or other."

"And there's lemon pie for dessert," Mom said. I thought that would certainly change his mind, but all he did was hold out his hand to Dave.

"So long, buddy. Take care," he said as they shook hands.

Dave walked out onto the front porch with Larry. When he came back a few minutes later, he was shaking his head. "That's funny. Larry acted as if he was running to put out a fire."

"Well, he is busy with all his volunteer jobs. And I guess he figured with all of us going to the depot, there wouldn't be any reason for him to tag along." Even as I spoke those words, a flash of intuition told me that's not what he figured at all. Dave was going into the service. He was a hero. And Larry? He was a 4F, doomed to stay home with the women and children and the men who were past their prime. Dave was going on to glory; Larry would be left in the shadows.

"Here's your pie, Dave. Time's getting short. Eat up." Mom's words struck me like a bomb blast: In just a little over an hour, Dave will be leaving. Tomorrow morning when I get up, he'll be miles away instead of sitting there across from me, kicking my ankles, driving me crazy with his goofy remarks.

Oh, Dave, I'll miss you, I started to say, but Dad was talking and then Doris said something and Dave answered her and the chance was gone.

Chapter 16

*S*IXTEEN. *I AM FINALLY SIXTEEN, A MAGICAL AGE, THE DIVIDING line between childhood and adulthood. In the space of one short day I have entered a new world that abounds with romance and challenges. Even as I reflect upon the difference that twenty-four hours has made in my life, the telephone rings. I answer its insistent call to hear the voice of an impatient suitor, the third that evening.*

"Marjorie, I've watched you from afar for lo, these many years, longing for you as you grew from an impish child to a charming young woman," he says. "Will you—oh, please say yes—will you accept my invitation to dinner and dancing this coming Saturday?"

I turned the pages of my appointment calendar. "Oh, I'd love to, but I'm busy that evening. Perhaps the week following?"

For as long as I could remember, I had wanted to be sixteen more than anything else in the world. Now here it was March twentieth and yesterday had been my birthday, but nothing had changed. Oh, my folks had given me a new watch and Doris some knee-length plaid socks, but I didn't feel any different, and there sure wasn't any line of boys waiting to take me out. Not that I would have dated anyone, because I really did love Prentice, but it would have been nice to have someone want to take me to a movie or something.

I think that Donnie from across the street would have asked me out, but Mom had told me not to stop and talk with any of the soldiers. "The neighbors would talk, dear," she said. "You have to protect your reputation."

My reputation, I was tempted to reply. What about my reputation as a wallflower, probably the only dateless sixteen-year-old in a town that was overflowing with lonely men? I was so starved for a social life that I would have been thrilled even to go to a movie with Doris, but she had an endless supply of excuses as to why she had to stay home on the weekends.

Finally, though, there was some excitement in my life—Dave was coming home on leave! His train would be arriving at eight o'clock on a Saturday morning in the middle of April. On that day, Mom rousted me out of bed at six so we could clean house before he got here. I thought we were going through an awful lot of trouble for someone who wouldn't recognize a dust ball if it came up and introduced itself, but there were no complaints from me as we scrubbed and mopped and vacuumed.

At 7:30 Dad drove off to pick Dave up. When 8:30 came and they weren't back yet, I started pacing the floor. "They should be here," I said. "What if something's happened? Maybe there's been a train wreck. Maybe his leave's been canceled." Maybe he's been shipped overseas, and no one told us. I MAY NEVER SEE MY BROTHER AGAIN! The words flashed into my head, so big, so threatening, that they blocked out any thought of Prentice or of Ellen. Just one more time I wanted to hear the sound of the screen door slamming behind him, wanted him to muss my hair and call me kid, wanted him to hog the bathroom, leaving me with no hot water for my shower. How intolerable those annoyances had once seemed to be; how precious they now appeared.

"Calm down." Mom rearranged the knickknacks on the buffet for what must have been the third time. "Trains are never on time these days." And then she went to the door and looked out onto the street as she'd been doing every two or three minutes for the last half hour.

Finally, at a little after nine, there were heavy footsteps on the front porch. "He's here!" I shouted as I ran to the door, eager to throw my arms around my big brother. But my arms stayed at my sides as I stared at someone who was a stranger, someone who was older, taller, thinner than Dave. There's a mistake, I thought, my heart fluttering with the beginnings of panic. Where's Dave?

And then the stranger grinned and I threw open the screen door. "It's you. Really you!"

"Hey, kid," he said, hugging me. "How are things going?"

I stood back to take a good look at him. "Okay, but the barber that got hold of you must have been in a really bad mood."

"I know." Dave ran his hand over his head just as Prentice had the first time I met him.

"Well, for heaven's sake, Marjorie," Mom said, "stand aside so I can give my son a welcome-home hug."

"And then let's get some food into him. Looks to me like the marines are giving him short rations." Dad pulled out his handkerchief and wiped his eyes. My father crying? The thought of his being so soft, so deeply moved, was completely foreign to me. If his tears were a sign of relief, was it possible that he had been plagued with the same uncertainties, the same feeling of emptiness that followed me about from day to day? The idea conflicted with the image I'd always had of my father—that of a sturdy, confident Rock of Gibraltar.

Dave laughed. "Oh, I get plenty to eat. It's just that sometimes I can't quite tell what it is."

"Buttermilk pancakes and bacon coming right up." Mom bustled off toward the kitchen.

"Doris will be here in a couple of hours," I said. "And Larry said he'd try to drop by in a little while. Tell me all about what it's like being a marine."

"A lot of yelling and marching and standing in line for chow." Dave stretched out on the couch. "Now that boot camp's over, it should get better."

"I got a letter from Ellen and one from Prentice on the same day last week. Ellen sounds like she's getting along all right. Her mom's working as a waitress."

Frowning, Dave sat up. "Wish Mrs. Altman would get out . . . but then, of course, it's hard not knowing whether her husband's dead or alive."

Not as hard as knowing he's dead. I felt a momentary tinge of antagonism at this woman I'd never met, but it disappeared when Dad walked into the room carrying his Brownie box camera. "Come on outside, Dave. There's just enough sun for a decent shot."

By the time the picture taking was over, Mom had put a big platterful of pancakes and crispy bacon on the table. "Pull up your chairs, everyone. Get it while it's hot." She stood back, arms folded, seeming to get her nourishment from watching Dave eat the food she'd prepared.

The four of us were still sitting around the table talking at 10:30 when Larry showed up. "Hey, buddy, great to see you," Dave said, slapping him on the back. Larry punched Dave in the arm, and I was struck by the thought that, while women hug, men slap and punch each other to show their affection. I suppose the important thing is the touching, no matter how it's done.

When Doris arrived an hour later, the room was filled with laughing and talking. There couldn't have been a happier place in the world than the Ellison front room. For the moment, at least, the war seemed very far away.

During the succeeding days of Dave's leave, the feverish, almost frantic tone of the day of his arrival changed to the quiet contentment of a family whose members take pleasure in just being together. Dad no longer took refuge in the evening radio news, but joined in the dinner-table conversation. Mom, in between urging Dave to take second and third helpings, told entertaining stories about the people and events at work. I usually sat quietly, absorbing the good feelings that filled the room, storing them up for the less happy times that were sure to come.

As the day of Dave's departure neared, the casual conversations took on an undertone of things unsaid. "Well, now Corregidor's fallen to the Japs." Dad's statement was matter-of-fact, but I felt that inside he was really saying, "Dave, how grateful I am that you weren't one of those killed at Bataan." And Mom would say something like, "I hope you won't be skipping breakfast. That's such an important meal." I had the strong sense that what she wanted to say was "Come back to us healthy and sound. Dear God, don't let me get one of those telegrams."

Sometimes during a break in the stream of chatter, the unspoken thoughts resonated in the stillness, and to silence them, I said whatever inconsequential thing that came into my mind. As a result, on the final day of his leave, as I watched Dave pack his bag, I realized how many important things I'd left unsaid. But, even then I couldn't come right out and declare "I love you. I miss you. The house is so empty and quiet without you." I couldn't voice any of those feelings. And even if I could, wouldn't I ruin the moment by blubbering and sniffling? Dave hates seeing anyone cry—I'd never forget the stricken, helpless look on his face the time he'd teased me to the point of tears. Never again had he stepped over the line that divides a lighthearted jest from hurtful ridicule.

"Do you know where you're going to be stationed?" I asked.

"Probably on some South Pacific island with a bunch of hula girls."

I hated the way he made light of the fact that he'd be going overseas, but to cover up my emotional state, I replied in kind. Twirling the fringe of his bedspread around my finger, I tilted my head and looked at him. "I bet you'd rather have Doris there than a hula girl."

"Hey there, getting a little personal, aren't you?" He crammed an olive-green undershirt into his bag, then started closing the buckles. "But to satisfy your curiosity—yes, I would." After a slight pause, he said, "And how about you and Prentice? You heard from him lately?"

My face grew warm, but I tried to sound casual. "He writes two or three times a week. I guess he likes me all right." I sighed. "I think about him a lot, especially on the weekends because there's nothing much to do."

"How about going someplace with Doris?"

I shrugged. "She never wants to do anything."

Dave sat down on the other end of the bed. "I've been meaning to do something about that. I'll try to talk her into taking you up on some of your invitations. She needs a friend . . . I mean *really* needs one . . . and I'd appreciate it if you'd sort of keep an eye on her while I'm gone."

"I'd be glad to." I grinned. "Since I'm going to be doing you such a big favor, maybe you'd want to send me a dollar or two once in a while . . . you know, for a movie or something."

Dave's expression remained serious. "Why not? This is important to me . . . it really is."

Why was it so important? I didn't ask the question. "Where is Doris anyway? Isn't she going to see you off?"

"Nope. We said good-bye last night." He stood up and slung his duffel bag over his shoulder. "Guess we better hit the road."

Good-bye. That's what war meant—saying good-bye. First to Ellen, now to Dave. Soon, maybe to Kaye. Good-bye was so much more final than "so long."

Mom and Dad didn't say much as we drove to the depot, but Dave and I kidded around just as if this were any ordinary day. Of course, it was hard to talk around the lump in my throat and once in a while I had to take a deep breath because my lungs felt so tight.

The train was waiting when we got there. It was full of servicemen, some of them sleeping, some just staring out of the windows. Mom and Dad took turns hugging Dave. Mom started to cry, but Dave chucked her under her chin and told her to stow the tears. Then he climbed aboard the next-to-the-last passenger car.

"All aboard!" The voice jarred me as I searched in vain for a glimpse of Dave in the crowded car. Then just as the train lurched forward, I saw him, leaning toward the smudged window, waving to us from the aisle. We all waved back as smoke puffed from the top of the locomotive and the wheels turned with a grinding, creaking protest.

"He doesn't even have a seat," Mom cried. "Does he have to stand all the way? The least they could do is give him a place to sit down."

"It's all right, Dorothy. I'm sure they'll find something for him." Dad's voice was strained, his face pale.

We stood there among the other friends and relatives of the departing servicemen as the train chugged down the track, slowly picking up speed. Dad gripped Mom's hand, as much, I thought, for his own support as for hers. The train appeared to grow small in the distance. Within five minutes all that was left was a lingering cloud of steam and the smell of grease. Dave was gone, and I looked down at the platform so no one would see the tears that flooded my face.

Chapter 17

*E*VER SINCE WE HAD ENTERED THE WAR, THE MAILBOX HAD assumed a monumental importance in my life. Now, with Dave gone, Mom and Dad also seemed to hold their breath each time they approached it, pulled down its metal door, and reached inside. When, six days after Dave's departure, there was a scrawled postcard from him, Dad's good humor radiated like heat from the floor furnace and Mom hummed a series of off-key tunes as she scraped the carrots and peeled the potatoes for dinner.

Doris told me that she had received a long letter from Dave, but didn't reveal any of its contents. On Friday night, though, she asked me if I wanted to go to a movie with her the next afternoon, and I knew that Dave must have convinced her to start going out. I would have preferred a visit to the Skating Palace, but sensed that if I suggested it, Doris might scuttle back into her shell and Dave would have to start all over again.

It was a little after three when we got out of the show. I was just about to ask her if she wanted to have a Coke at Kress's lunch counter when casually, catching me completely off guard, Doris invited me to come to her apartment to meet her mother. Mrs. Altman! I finally had the chance to meet this mystery woman, but now that the moment had arrived, I hesitated.

"Well?" Doris said, snapping and unsnapping the latch on her purse, and I had the impression this was more Dave's idea than it was hers.

"It's just that Mom's expecting me to come home right after the movie."

"Oh. Well, maybe some other time." Doris sounded relieved. I knew if I didn't take her up on this invitation, there would never be another one.

"But I could call her from your place, I guess. She'll understand." Yes, she'll understand because ever since Dave had started dating Doris, she'd been curious about Mrs. Altman, too.

Doris's face tightened. "It's up to you."

"Let's go," I said, and a moment later we were running to catch the North Park streetcar. As we rode, Doris alternated between staring out the window, saying nothing, and babbling about Dave and about a school she used to attend and about how she hated gym class. As she talked, she kept snapping and unsnapping that latch on her purse until I was sure it would break off.

When we got off the streetcar at Park and El Cajon and started walking south, Doris lapsed into another silence. "Wasn't Greer Garson perfect in the movie?" I said. "There she was, calm and brave with bombs falling all over the place and not knowing what happened to her son."

"That's not the way it is, you know," Doris said, looking straight ahead.

"What do you mean?"

"People don't act that way in real life." She led the way into a shabby-looking apartment building, and something in her demeanor warned me not to pursue the subject. So many times when I was with her, I had the sense of walking in a mine field, stepping carefully, afraid of setting off an explosion.

We walked down a dimly lit, musty smelling hall to a door marked 3. Doris rapped softly, then harder. No answer. She hesitated, then dug in her purse and pulled out a key. "She must be resting . . . that's it . . . she gets tired a lot." She mumbled the words, almost as if she were trying to convince herself instead of me.

I followed her into the small front room of the apartment. The air smelled stale, and the coffee table was covered with magazines and unfolded newspapers. Through the open kitchen door I could see a few dirty dishes and several empty beer bottles on the counter. Doris pushed the door shut. "Mom must have had someone over. She never—"

She was interrupted by a moan that came from what must have been one of the bedrooms. Doris threw her purse down and muttered, "Oh, no. She promised." Pushing past me, she peered into the room. "My gosh," she gasped.

With my hand on Doris's shoulder, I took my first look at Doris's mother. She was lying beside the bed, her long brown hair spread out on the floor. She was so still that if she hadn't been moaning, I'd have thought she was dead. "Is she all right?" I whispered as Doris dropped to her knees and leaned over her.

Doris nodded. "I guess so. I don't know. She's never passed out before." She looked up at me, her face twisted, tears running down her cheeks. "She promised . . . she knew I was going to ask you over . . . and she promised she wouldn't drink."

Awed by my first close contact with a drunk person, I said the first thing that came into my mind. "Does this happen a lot?" I knew immediately I should have kept my mouth shut.

"Of course not." Doris's eyes flashed as she stood up. "It's only since Daddy . . . since Daddy . . ." A sudden new gush of tears choked off her words, but a moment later she found her voice again. "I told you not everyone can be like your precious Mrs. Miniver." She looked down at her mother. "You better go home. It was dumb of me to let you come here. But she did promise. She really did."

I wanted to get out of that place more than anything else in the world, but couldn't get my feet to move toward the door. "You can't leave her lying there on the floor. Shouldn't we try to get her up on the bed?"

Doris wiped her eyes with the sleeve of her sweater, then shook her mother's shoulder. "Mom, can you hear me?"

Mrs. Altman's eyes flickered and she pushed Doris's hand away. "Lea . . . me . . . lone," she muttered.

"Here," I said, moving into the room. "You take her hands and I'll take her feet. When I count to three, lift."

We managed to get Mrs. Altman onto the bed on the second try. "What do we do now?" I asked. "Shouldn't we bring her to?"

Doris shrugged.

"I saw this movie once," I said. "A man had too much to drink and his friend threw cold water in his face to sober him up."

Doris looked at her mother, then at me. "Do you really think we should?"

"Well, it sure worked in the movie. That guy was back on his feet real quick."

"Let's do it." Doris went into the kitchen, returned with a pitcher full of water, and handed it to me, seeming to relinquish the responsibility for the care of the woman on the bed. I stood there, wavering, realizing that this treatment may not be the one most doctors would recommend.

"Here, you do it," I said, shoving the pitcher at Doris, who took it, then stood there like a statue in a fountain, dribbling water on the floor.

And then I got the giggles—the worst case I'd ever had in my entire life. Wave after wave of chuckles and chortles welled up inside me and spilled out as I clutched my stomach and tried to hold them back; they kept coming and then Doris joined in, not just giggling but laughing out loud, while water sloshed around her in a semicircle. Between spasms, I took the pitcher from her and placed it on the nightstand, then we staggered into the front room and plopped down on the sagging couch.

A couple of minutes passed before I could speak. "Guess we'd better just let her sleep it off," I said.

Doris took off her glasses and wiped her eyes with the back of her hand. "You're right. If she woke up and found the bed soaked, there's no telling what she'd do to me." She grinned—not the hesitant little smile I'd become used to—but a real ear-to-ear grin. "Boy, I bet you'll never forget your first visit to the Altmans."

"You are so right."

Doris suddenly sat up straight, then leaned toward me, her eyes dark, her body rigid. "Don't tell anyone. Not *anyone*. You have to promise." The laughing, lighthearted girl was gone. In her place was the Doris I was accustomed to—unsmiling, somber, intense.

"Why should I tell anyone?" I reached for my purse, feeling uncomfortable, knowing that it was time for me to leave.

"But you have to promise . . . say it."

"All right, I promise."

"This is my fault, you know. I shouldn't have left her alone. She can't help it . . . she's so worried about Daddy and so lonely . . ."

It's *not* your fault, I wanted to say. Instead I stood up and reached for the doorknob. "I'll call you later," I said. "Let's make plans for next weekend. You been to the zoo yet?"

Doris shook her head. "No, not yet. But before I make any plans I'd better wait and see how Mom is."

As I walked down the hall, my mind was buzzing with images and impressions—the dreary apartment, Mrs. Altman lying there on the floor, the stricken look on Doris's face, the two of us giggling until we were completely giggled out, Doris carrying the burden of guilt for her mother's actions.

Does Dave know about this? I wondered. Probably. So, is this why he takes her out—because he feels sorry for her? I hoped not, because that wouldn't be the least bit fair, either to Doris or himself.

On the other hand, maybe he'd seen some things in Doris that I had never seen until this afternoon. The way she's been taking care of her mother without complaint. The volunteer work in which she was involved. And all this time waiting for news about her father. Waiting for the mailman. Afraid whenever she saw a Western Union messenger in her neighborhood. Yes, Dave must have seen that Doris is a special person. How would *I* act if I had all those problems? I wondered. Would I be like Doris, or like Mrs. Miniver? Or would I fall to pieces like Mrs. Altman?

"My mother is in a tuberculosis sanitarium and my father is laid up with a broken leg," I told the school counselor. "I have no choice but to quit school and go to work to support my family."

The counselor placed her hand upon mine. "Such courage. Such dedication. But my dear, you must stay in school. You're such a brilliant scholar. Why, that essay on Shakespeare was . . ."

I waved her praise aside. "I want nothing more than to complete my education, but my family must come first."

The admiration in the counselor's eyes made me uncomfortable. I was, after all, only doing my duty.

* * *

The streetcar rattled to a stop and I climbed aboard, suddenly remembering that I had forgotten to call my mother. She'll be worried about me, I thought. She'll be putting some rice pudding in the oven or making some spaghetti sauce, and she'll be wondering what's keeping me. And when I get home she'll be upset with me and she'll tell me to set the table and, for once, I won't mind even one little bit.

Chapter 18

*A*FTER DAVE HAD SAILED FROM SAN FRANCISCO ON A TROOP ship, our dining room took on the air of a military command post. On one wall Dad had hung a big world map that was now dotted with thumb tacks—white for the Allied forces and black for the Axis. Every evening after he had finished reading the *San Diego Sun* and listened to the news on the radio, he moved the pins around to show the day's military movements. None of us dared speak to him while he completed what had become an almost sacred ritual.

It pained me to look at the left-hand side of that map because there were so many more black pins than white. Japan was no longer a quaint group of islands on the other side of the ocean— it was a rampaging monster that devoured everything in its path. Manila, Malaya, Borneo, Singapore, Bali, Rangoon—all the exotic places I'd seen in Dorothy Lamour kinds of movies were in enemy hands or were about to be overcome. It was the same with Guam and Wake Island and dozens of other bits of land that had only recently become known to me.

Ellen and I were still best friends, writing to each other every other day. She had met another sailor, whom she liked about as much as she liked Jack, but she wasn't going to tell Jack until she was more sure of her feelings. I thought that was a good idea. A "Dear John" letter would almost certainly shatter a serviceman's morale and send him into battle with no will to survive.

She didn't say much about missing her father, but I had become an expert at reading between the lines. "The other day," she wrote in one letter, "Mom told me we might stay in Honolulu after the war's over. I'd like that." (So she can be close to her father, I surmised.) "Of course," she continued, "I'd hate not seeing you, but who knows, maybe you can come to see *me*."

And I will, I promised myself. With all the women going into war work, I can get all the baby-sitting jobs I want, if Dad will only let me, or maybe I can work in a soda shop during the summer and save all my money. Meanwhile, I was spending a lot of my spare time with Doris—so much time, in fact, that there wasn't much time left for the Narasakis. Then on a balmy Saturday evening in late March, Kaye called me with some chilling news.

"Marjorie, it's awful. Just a little while ago these soldiers banged at our door . . . we were so scared . . . and they showed us some official papers. In forty-eight hours they're sending a truck to pick us up. Forty-eight hours! Can you believe it? And they wouldn't even tell us where they're taking us."

"Kaye, how awful. What about your store . . . your apartment . . . all your things?"

"We'll just have to take what we can and leave the rest. No time to do anything." Her voice broke.

"I'll come down and help you pack." What a feeble offer of assistance after all those weeks of neglect.

"No, no," Kaye said. "Mom's so upset . . . she doesn't like anyone to see her when she might start crying any minute. I'll write to you when we get settled." She paused. When she continued, her voice was soft, yet steady. "Marjorie, you've been a good friend. We'll never forget you."

But I haven't been a friend, not really, I protested silently. You've been, but not me. My throat filled with tears, and I had to push my reply through them. "I'll write as soon as I hear from you. I'll miss you so much." The tears were rising. I could feel their pressure against the backs of my eyes.

"Marjorie, do you suppose you could sort of watch the store for us? There's no one else I can ask."

I grasped at this chance to make up for my thoughtlessness. "Oh, yes. I promise. It'll be right there waiting for you when you get back."

"See you after the war, then." Kaye's laugh was shaky.

"Are you sure you don't want me to come down? I want to see you. I really do."

"Same here, but you know Mom. She's so . . . well, I guess it's pride or something, but those guys made her and Papa feel like criminals or something. She's so embarrassed. It would just hurt her more if she had to face you."

"Okay, but don't forget to write."

"I won't. So long." And then I heard the finality of the dial tone.

I put the receiver back on its hook, tempted to ignore Kaye's pleas for me to stay away, feeling ashamed because I'd already stayed away too much. I turned to Mom, who looked up from the sock she was darning. "That was Kaye," I said. "The Narasakis are being relocated." The tears had found their way to the fronts of my eyes, and I had to blink fast to hold them back.

Mom put her mending in her lap, her expression filled with dismay. "Oh, how terrible for them."

"They just got a couple of days' notice. How can they move in that little bit of time?"

Dad looked at me over the top of a *Liberty* magazine. "The point isn't whether they have time to move. The point is that if we give them any longer, they'll go around committing sabotage or spying or heaven only knows what."

Mom's jaw tightened and she pressed her lips together before she spoke. "I can't imagine that gentle man and woman doing those things."

"They wouldn't. I know they wouldn't," I said.

"Maybe not," Dad mumbled as he turned back to his reading. "But Roosevelt's right. We just can't take a chance."

I looked out the window. Now that the blackout had been lifted, the city lights were sparkling again, but tonight the view did nothing to soothe me. Maybe they'll be better off, I thought. It must have been awful lately—all those dirty looks, those slurs, the customers who weren't coming into their store anymore. But it should be *their* choice to leave, not some government agency with the power to force innocent people from their homes.

About a week after the Narasakis left, I got my first letter from Kaye: ". . . and we're living in a race track near Los Angeles," she wrote, "living in a *stable* . . ."

> *Stables must be great for horses, but they're awful for people. Mom and I have scrubbed and scrubbed, but they still smell, and there are still hundreds of flies.*
>
> *Dad never complains, but he seems to get weaker every day. He misses his own bed and worries about all the things we had to leave behind. My heart breaks a little bit every time I look at him. And of course, we're all*

worried about Paul. I can't believe they sent him to the South Pacific instead of to Europe. It seems to me it would be really easy for one of our own guys to shoot him by mistake. Or maybe it wouldn't be a mistake. I'm glad you're writing to him. He says it helps him to know that you're still his friend.

Sorry I couldn't write a more cheerful letter. I'll try to do better next time.

Your friend,
Kaye

P.S. *Thanks again for looking after our place.*

Kaye

I folded the letter and slipped it back into the envelope, thinking of the boarded-up building I had been visiting every day. It was already getting a run-down look, even though I had weeded the garden a couple of times and picked up some trash someone had thrown into the yard. One of the problems was that the water was shut off so the sweet pea vine was withering and the rosebushes were drooping. I'll haul some water down there, I decided. Even if I can't do much else, I can try to save those flowers.

At 7:30 the morning after I got Kaye's letter, Larry and I were walking to the bus stop and I was telling him about my plan to save Mrs. Narasaki's garden. When we turned the corner at the bottom of the hill, I glanced toward the store, blinked my eyes, then stared. It couldn't be! My stomach churned and for a moment I was afraid I'd lose my breakfast. Grabbing Larry's arm for support, I gasped. "My gosh, look . . . I can't believe it . . . just look."

The two of us stood there not speaking, overcome by what was facing us. The front and sides of the store were covered with great

smears of black paint that spelled out the words JAP DEVILS, TRAI-
TORS, FIFTH COLUMNISTS. Huge gobs of greasy-looking muck had
been spattered on the boards over the windows on the lower floor.
The boards on one side window had been ripped off. On the side
of the yard that was visible, the pansies and marigolds had been
trampled and uprooted, the same flowering plants that Mrs. Narasaki had tended so lovingly.

I walked over to the store and saw that the unprotected window
had been shattered. The rays of the sun revealed that the display
cases had been overturned and more ugly words smeared on the
walls.

Larry touched my shoulder. "The bus is coming," he said.

His gentle words startled me into action. "But I'm not going.
I have to clean this up. I promised Kaye . . ." Even I could hear
that my words were tinged with hysteria, but I *did* have to stay
here. I *couldn't* leave this mess.

"Let it be for now, Marjorie," Larry said, taking my arm and
leading me across the street. The bus stopped and we climbed on
and took our seats. A few seconds later the conversation going on
directly behind us penetrated the confused jumble of my thoughts.
". . . awful." It was a woman voice. "Why would anyone do a
thing like that?"

"It's obvious, isn't it?" a man said. "Damned Japs are just
getting what's coming to them."

Larry turned to look at the man. "You don't know what you're
talking about. Those people never hurt anyone."

I stared straight ahead, knowing that everyone on the bus was
staring at us. For a moment my embarrassment took the edge off
my anger, but then, like a flint striking a stone, the thought of
that ravaged building sparked an even stronger outrage. Twisting

in my seat, I fired off a volley of my own. "No one has a right to go around messing up other people's property. The Narasakis don't deserve . . ."

"Well, what do we have here? Two Jap lovers." The man's face was twisted, making him look as ugly as his words. "Is that why you're not in uniform?" he said to Larry. "Any red-blooded American boy would be out fighting the Nips, not sitting here sticking up for them." He looked around at the other passengers as if asking for approval. Most of them suddenly became interested in watching the traffic on the street, but I saw two older men nod their heads in silent agreement.

"Hey, you kids, quiet down back there or you'll have to get off the bus," the driver called. Not a word of warning to that loud-mouthed man, just to Larry and me. Larry turned to face the front of the bus, his jaws clenched, his eyes cold. He didn't even say anything when the man rose to get off at Laurel Street and muttered "Damn traitors," his expression seething with hate. For the first time in my life, I knew what it was like to be the target of ignorance. I had just experienced once what Kaye and her family must have experienced dozens of times over the past four months.

"Sorry I put you through that," Larry said after the bus had started moving again. "But some people really get under my skin."

"He's the one who should be sorry, not you." Although I was relieved the incident was over, I was grateful to have shared it with him, and I was grateful, too, that I had found the courage to support him even though that support had been weak and late in coming. But the next time, I'll be ready with the conviction of a real crusader.

Having captured the full attention of my audience, like an evangelical preacher I turned on the full power of my persuasive tongue.

"No, the Narasakis are not traitors. The traitors are those who persecute innocent people simply because they have skin of a different color. The traitors are the people who vandalize homes and places of business in the name of patriotism. The traitors are the men and women who skulk around in the dead of night, hiding behind the American flag to do their dastardly deeds, the ones who . . ."

Yes, the next time the opportunity arises, I'll make up for all the times I should have done something or said something to right a wrong but didn't. That's the least I can do for you, Kaye—the very least.

Chapter 19

ON THE FOLLOWING SATURDAY, LARRY AND I SPENT ALMOST ten hours trying to repair the damage that had been done to the Narasakis' place. While he painted over all the ugly words and replaced the boards over the broken window, I saved as much of the garden as I could. By the time we were through, my body ached in places that had never ached before, but the building no longer shouted its message of hate.

At six o'clock we put the paint buckets and brushes and hand tools in my old Radio Flyer wagon, then I picked up the hoe and shovel and we started toward home. My leg muscles complained as they carried me up the hill, but my sense of satisfaction dulled the pain.

"Good day's work," I said.

"Sure was. Now let's hope it doesn't happen again." He pushed his hair out of his eyes, leaving a smudge across his forehead.

"You're a mess, you know that?" I laughed. "Half paint and half dirt."

"Ha!" he said, pointing to my slacks. "You're bringing at least half of that garden home with you." He stopped to change hands on the wagon handle. "I'm glad we got this all done today. To-morrow I have to work on two term papers."

"I can't believe school will be out in just a few more weeks."

"I can't believe I'm going to be graduating," Larry said. "Guess it'll be San Diego State for me in the fall."

"What are you going to do this summer?" I asked.

"Work at Consolidated. How about you?"

"I don't know. When I told Dad I wanted to get a job, he told me he didn't think much of the idea. Said that he and Mom need me to take care of the house." I sighed. "My only hope is that Mom will talk him into it. It'd sure be nice to have some money. Dad has no idea how hard it is to buy a bus pass and clothes and stuff on my five-dollar-a-week allowance." We had reached Guy Street now and the air bore the delicate scent of our neighbor's honeysuckle bushes. Prentice—Prentice. I need to see you, to touch you, to hear your voice.

When we reached our driveway, Larry parked the wagon, positioning its wheels so it wouldn't roll down into our backyard. "Think it would help if I put in a good word for you?" he asked.

"What . . . ?" My mind had drifted away from the anchor of our conversation. "Oh . . . no, I think I'll have to depend upon whatever magic Mom can perform. But thanks anyway."

"Want me to put this stuff away?" Larry took the garden tools from me.

"No, it's okay. I'll do it later." I had to be alone to recapture the moment when Prentice's lips had touched mine.

But Larry didn't leave. He placed the tools against the side of the house, then gazed at the bay, his eyes pensive. "I had a good time today," he said.

"So did I." It *had* been a good day, the two of us working together, doing something constructive for a family whose dreams were being destroyed. In the end maybe our efforts wouldn't mean much, but at this moment, I had no doubt that we'd done something right in a world in which so many things were going wrong.

Larry said so long, then walked away. I watched him, feeling that as we had painted and scrubbed and pulled the weeds that had been choking the sweet peas, a very special bond of friendship had been created between us. And I thought again of that man on the bus, remembering that he had attacked not only the Narasakis but Larry also, and I hadn't said one single word in his defense.

There was no more vandalism over the next few weeks, maybe because whoever did the damage had vented their rage, maybe because there was so much good war news. A colonel named Jimmy Doolittle led a group of B-25's in a daring bombing raid on Tokyo, and we won an important battle in the Coral Sea and recaptured Midway.

"Now we're showing 'em," Dad mumbled whenever he pulled a black pin from his map and replaced it with a white one.

While I was as glad as he was that the tide seemed to be turning in our favor, a chill passed through me each time an island was recaptured or an enemy ship sunk. Those victories, after all, meant that lives had been lost. Where's Dave—where's Prentice? Are they all right? No matter how great the news from the front was, it was still the mail that determined whether the mood around our house was festive or gloomy. One Thursday we had a particular reason to celebrate—the mailman had brought not one, not two, but *three* letters from Dave. Dad's usual staid demeanor was transformed into such a carefree exuberance that he forgot to turn on the Philco for the six o'clock news.

"Dave says he wants some of your cherry cobbler, Dorothy." He grinned as he turned the page of the letter over. "Says he met some guy he knew in school. He wants to know how we're holding up. What a boy . . . worrying about us when he's facing God knows what out there."

Mom and I had already read every word in those letters, but as Dad repeated them, we grinned at each other, sharing his joy. How good it was to see his eyes sparkle and the weariness leave his face. Again, I had a sudden image of Dad as a young man, of the way he must have looked when he and Mom were dating, before he'd lost the spring in his step—before he'd realized he'd spend the rest of his life as an ordinary workman, struggling to pay his bills.

By the time Mom poured Dad's second cup of coffee, the mood around the table was so relaxed I dared to bring up the idea of my going to work during summer vacation. "I read in the paper that Consolidated is still hiring." I glanced at Mom, pleading for support, then turned back to Dad. "I don't want this whole war to go by without doing anything to help. And just think, I could buy all my own school clothes." I stopped, marshaling my other arguments.

But before I had a chance to say anything else, Mom was there, backing me up. "I can't help thinking how proud Dave would be with all of us working to get him back home sooner."

Nothing else was said until Dad finished his coffee. As he placed the cup on the saucer, he stroked his chin. "Well, how can I say no when you put it that way? If they can find something for a youngster to do, well . . ."

I jumped up and gave him a hug. "Dad, you're the greatest. I promise you . . . I'll do the best job ever."

"You better, or else." Dad's voice was gruff, but he hugged me back.

Me with a real grown-up job—a war job! Just wait till I tell Prentice about *this*.

* * *

Larry had already planned to apply for work the following Saturday morning, so I asked him if I could tag along with him. When we arrived at the crowded employment office, we got in line to get our applications, maneuvered our way to an empty space at the counter and filled them out, stood in another line to turn them in, then sat down together in the back of the room. An hour of waiting and Larry's encouragement about my chances of being hired had had a calming effect on my jumpy nerves. Now, however, we had run out of things to talk about and I was convinced that our papers had been lost and that we'd have to come back here next Saturday and go through the same procedure all over again and that maybe Dad had been right all along and my getting a job wasn't such a good idea.

A grizzled-looking old man passed in front of us to take a seat and I wondered how many dreary employment offices he had visited over the years. Judging from the way he slumped into the chair there must have been dozens, and he'd probably been rejected as often as he'd been hired. But the war had brought an end to the long depression—the country needed all the war workers it could get. My dad finally had a good job, and Mom had been hired with no experience, and this man would be, too, and so would I. Yes, even me, a sixteen-year-old girl.

To while away the time, I concentrated on reading the posters that hung on the side walls. "I'll give 'em hell if you give me the stuff," said a rugged-looking, helmeted soldier who was holding a bayonet. Another pictured a hand squeezing a snake that had a Japanese face. "It's a fight to the finish," read the caption on that one. A third poster pictured three women. Even wearing overalls and with their hair up in snoods and nets, they looked like movie stars. "Soldiers without guns" they were called.

A soldier. That's what I'll be when I start working here. A civilian soldier. Why, I could even be put to work on some secret project—maybe a new kind of weapon.

The enemy agents who had bound and gagged me took me to what appeared to be an underground cavern—a dank, foul-smelling place. Now I was surrounded by evil-looking men in Japanese army uniforms. "Give us the information we seek," one of them said. "If you persist in being stubborn . . ." He didn't have to finish the statement. The murderous look in his beady eyes gave me a clear picture of his intentions.

"Do to me what you will," I said in a trembling voice. "I'll never betray my country."

A red-hot poker was brought close to my face. Exhaustion overtook me, and I started to slide into oblivion. Through the fog that surrounded me, I heard my name being called again and again . . .

"Marjorie Ellison. Is Marjorie Ellison here?"

Larry shook my arm. "Hey, you asleep or something? They're calling you."

I jumped up, stumbled over the feet of the man sitting between me and the aisle, and hurried to the counter, straightening my wrinkled skirt, trying to look composed and competent. The woman frowned as she read my application.

"Just turned sixteen, I see. So many kids coming in nowadays. Most of 'em don't know what real work is." She looked up from the paper. "Can you show up for work every day?"

"I hardly ever miss school," I replied in a quavering, subdued voice.

"No experience, huh?"

"Well, no, I never worked . . ."

"I'll file your application." The woman's eyes were cold as she dismissed me. "We'll let you know if anything comes up." Glancing at the next application, she bellowed, "Woods! Larry Woods!"

"But—but . . ." My protest was futile. I turned to see that Larry was already striding up to the counter. As I passed him on the way back to my seat, I looked beyond him, knowing if I saw any sympathy in his eyes, I'd burst into tears and wouldn't Miss Hatchet-face love *that*.

Then, as if I wasn't feeling miserable enough, the next voice I heard was that of Beverly Rhodes. "Marjorie! Imagine meeting you here. So you're going to work at Consolidated, too. How simply great."

I looked up and forced a smile. "Oh, hi." At least I had the satisfaction of knowing that her chance of getting a job was even less than mine. After all, one look at those manicured nails and those lotioned hands and Miss Hatchet-face would know that this girl wasn't cut out to be an aircraft assembler. I pointed to the other side of the room. "That's where you get in line to get an application."

"But I've already been hired. Daddy knows someone who works in the office and he called up and got me a job just like that." She snapped her fingers. "I'm just down here today to fill out a couple of papers and get my badge."

Just then Larry walked toward us holding some papers. "Well, Bev, does this mean you're spending your vacation at Consolidated, too?"

Beverly's giggle grated on my nerves like sandpaper. "I sure am. In the office. I know I'll love it." She giggled again. "Maybe we can all eat lunch together."

Before Larry had a chance to answer, I stood up. "We'd better hurry. I'm supposed to meet Doris in an hour."

"Sure," Larry said. "See you later, Bev."

We walked out of the office, through the main gate, and across Pacific Coast Highway, me feeling devastated, Larry oblivious to my misery. Finally, when I was almost home, I dredged up the courage to tell him I hadn't been hired.

"I kind of figured that when they didn't give you any employment papers," Larry said. "But don't give up. They'll probably call you in a couple of days."

"Not if Miss Hatchet-face has any say in the matter."

"Who?" Larry laughed. "Oh, you mean that gal at the counter. Good name. But even if you don't get on here, there are plenty of other places. How about Rohr in Chula Vista? By bus, you'd make it out there in less than thirty minutes from downtown."

"If Consolidated wouldn't take me, why would any other aircraft factory be interested?"

"Maybe the people at Rohr might have better sense than Miss Hatchet-face."

To hide my blush, I bent over the mailbox and pulled out an envelope. "It's from Kaye," I said. "Want to hear what she says?"

"Sure." Larry sat on the steps as I opened the letter and started to read.

Dear Marjorie,

Paul's overseas, in constant danger of being killed by both Americans and Japanese soldiers. We've lost our home and our business. But all this is nothing compared to what I must now tell you. My dear, dear father passed away four days ago. Now it's my turn to hate, because I know with a certainty that if we hadn't been sent to this terrible place, he'd still be alive.

Mother, of course, is inconsolable. Nothing I can do or say can break through her grief.

153

I feel that my father is as much a casualty of this war as any soldier killed on a battlefield, but for him, of course, there will be no medals, no memorial ceremonies . . .

Tears blurred my vision. I stopped reading. Larry stood up and took my hand, and I put my head on his chest, sobbing, my heart breaking as I grieved for that gentle, soft-spoken man who had answered a pesky little girl's million-and-one questions. Why hadn't I ever thanked him? Now the chance was gone forever.

Chapter 20

THE SHADOW OF MR. NARASAKI'S DEATH HUNG OVER ME AS I took my final exams in school and even during Larry's graduation exercises. Everything I did was tainted with anger and grief and the persistent painful awareness that I'd never be able to turn the clock back and do all the things I should have done, or say any of the things I should have said. Mom seemed to understand my torment, and I know Larry did, but I had to hide it from Dad and Doris and Ellen. To them, having one less Japanese in the world was a blessing, not a burden.

Now summer vacation was coming up, and for the first time in my life, I dreaded the thought of not having any school bells to parcel up my day, no homework to occupy my evenings, nothing to justify my getting out of bed in the morning. Doris would be busy at the hospital; Mom and Dad and Larry and even Beverly Rhodes would be working at Consolidated; and me?—instead of being a civilian soldier I'd be a drone with nothing to do but make beds and iron and dust, with "Stella Dallas" and "Ma Perkins" keeping me company on the radio.

Then on Saturday morning—one week after school had let out—just like in the movies, everything changed like magic, because I got a postcard from Consolidated. "If you're still available for

155

work," it said, "report to the personnel office at 7 A.M. on Monday, June 23." In the same mail, there was a letter from Prentice and one from Ellen, who was spending the summer working in a bakery—she hoped she wouldn't eat too many doughnuts and get fat. How grateful I was that she had set such a lighthearted tone for our correspondence. It relieved me of the obligation to ask her how she was coping with her father's death; or how her mother was handling her widowhood; or what it was like to wake up on a Sunday morning to a world gone mad. Now, I could write to her about all the little ordinary things that had made up our lives before December seventh, the day our world had changed so abruptly.

Prentice said he was laid up with a broken ankle he'd gotten when he was on patrol. I was relieved to hear that, at least for a little while, he'd be away from any battle zone, but when he told me about the cute nurses who were taking care of him, I wondered if I meant as much to him as he did to me.

I pushed the worrisome thought aside. Right now I had to talk to Dad about getting an advance on my allowance, then go downtown to buy an aircraft worker's uniform. How proud I'll feel when I'm wearing it, I thought. Everyone who sees me will know that I'm doing my part to win this war.

When Monday morning came, I felt more nervous than proud. As I followed Larry through Consolidated's main gate, my cornflakes and banana were sitting like a rock in my stomach, and I knew it would be a miracle if I didn't get fired before the week was out.

"Don't worry," Larry said, opening the door to the personnel office. "They hardly ever bite anyone. Wish I could stay with you, but it's getting late. See you at lunch." He walked across the asphalt pathway and joined the men and women who were lined up to punch in on the time clock. I stood there watching him, feeling as abandoned as I had when Dad had taken me to kindergarten for the first time, then left me alone with a bunch of kids I'd never seen before and a teacher who kept calling me Gertrude instead of Marjorie.

Miss Hatchet-face was working behind the counter when I walked into the employment office. Steeling myself against her harsh tongue, I handed her the notification card I'd received in the mail. "Ellison, Ellison," she murmured, sorting through a pile of papers. There's been a mistake, I thought. I knew it. I knew it all along. Just as I had convinced myself that I might as well turn and run, she pulled out one of the sheets of paper and glanced at it. "Here it is." She handed me some forms. "Fill these out." Miss Hatchet-face certainly didn't waste any words.

Five minutes later, I again approached the counter and waited silently for more instructions. Finally Miss Hatchet-face noticed me and took my employment papers. Frowning, she looked through them while I stood there feeling as if she were one of my teachers grading my final exam. Would I fail her careful scrutiny, or would I pass?

I must have passed, because she put the forms in a drawer and handed me a badge. "Wear this at all times," she said. "Now report to Department D." There was no hint of warmth in her eyes, but also no sign of recognition, for which I was grateful.

"Where's Depart—?" My question lay hanging in the air when she turned to help someone else. I left the office, walked across the pathway, hesitated, then headed toward the open entrance of the huge building that faced me. As I stepped from the asphalt onto the cement floor of the factory, I was deluged by a cacophony of jarring sounds echoing off the gray walls and high ceilings—

hammers hitting metal, drills buzzing in various pitches, machines clumping, whirring, hissing, clacking, clanging. Bedlam—that was the word that described this frightening, alien place.

An overalled workman walked past me as if I were invisible. A balding man pushing a dolly loaded with boxes rushed by in the other direction. No one looked my way. No one smiled a greeting. There I stood, my hair tucked neatly into a net, wearing a badge that affirmed my right to be here, wishing that I were back home listening to "The Romance of Helen Trent" on the radio.

Then, just as I was going to turn around and head toward the gate, the heroic image of the women on the poster replaced that of the clerk's grim countenance. A soldier without a gun—that's what I had dreamed of being—that was what I was *going* to be, no matter what anyone else thought. Standing straight, with resolute steps, I strode up to a grandmotherly looking woman and waited until she put her riveting gun down. "Where's Department D?" I shouted through her protective mask.

She pointed to my left and shouted back, "Through those doors. In the next building."

"Thanks." Clutching my purse to keep my hands from trembling, I dodged a man who hurried past me with a bunch of long rods over his shoulder and stepped to one side when a motorized cart sped toward me. When I had finally made my way to Department D, I approached a man who was seated on a high stool in front of a tall wooden desk. "Excuse me," I said in a tiny, apologetic voice.

"Yeah?" The man glared at me over the top of his horn-rimmed glasses.

"I'm suppose to start work here today." I handed him my card.

He took off his glasses and slid down from the stool. "Guess I can find something for you to do. Boy, they're hiring 'em younger every day."

I knew I must look like a twelve-year-old with my hair pulled back with a net and my uniform slacks and top baggy where they should be filled out, and just the barest touch of lipstick, but I resented his disparaging attitude.

"Don't be nervous, kid." The man's faced relaxed in a half-grin. "By the way, I'm Pat, your leadman, and I don't give a darn how old you are if you show up every day and get the job done." He led me to a workbench and introduced me to a chubby girl with strands of curly blond hair peeking out from her bandanna. "Arlene, this is Marjorie. Put her to work sorting rivets."

"Hi." Arlene put down her drill and turned to face me. I was surprised to see that even though she couldn't have been more than seventeen or eighteen years old, there was a gold band on her left ring finger. "Here, take this can of rivets and sort them out accordin' to size." She grinned. "Most of the jobs around here aren't what y'all might call glamorous."

Truer words had never been spoken. By 9:30 I had already sorted enough rivets to build at least a dozen bombers and a few fighter planes to boot, and a gray-haired man in patched overalls had just put another can in front of me. When the buzzer sounded for the mid-morning break, I rubbed the small of my back in a futile effort to relax my knotted muscles.

"Sorta achy?" Arlene asked. "That's 'cause you slump. Gotta keep your back straight while you work."

"Thanks. I'll remember that. Have you been here long?"

She shook her head. "Just a coupla' months. I came out here from Texas when my Earl got transferred."

"Earl . . . is that your husband?"

"Yep. Met him at a U.S.O. dance seven months ago." She twisted the ring around her finger and sighed. "Couldn't wait to tie the knot, we were that much in love."

"You're lucky. My boyfriend's in the marines and we never even had a chance to be alone before he left, except for a couple of hours." That walk to the Orchid. That kiss.

Arlene frowned. "You might think it's great to be hitched, but sometimes I wish I'd listened to my mama. When I think of all the fun I used to have, and now here I am, with Earl up in those Aleutian Islands, and me here in Dago with no one." She looked down at the floor for a second. "I tell you, with all these guys around, I'm sorely tempted to step out once in a while."

"But you wouldn't, would you? I mean, you're married."

"Haven't cheated yet, but who knows what'll happen if the war goes on and on?"

The break was over. It was time to go back to what must have been the most boring job at Consolidated Aircraft. As I worked, I wondered if I was going to spend the whole summer sifting through cans of rivets, placing them into the compartments of trays, never being given the chance to do anything important, unnoticed, unrecognized. . . .

In response to a tap on my shoulder, I looked up from my work to find myself gazing into the eyes of a broad-shouldered marine lieutenant. "Marjorie Ellison?" he said.

"Yes?" I replied, noting the rows of campaign ribbons that adorned his jacket.

"Your country needs you." His voice was deep and resonant. "We have intercepted some Japanese messages and are having trouble decoding them.

You must come with me immediately. I've already told your superiors that you'd be leaving."

Everyone in the department was staring at us as we walked out of the building. And just as we passed through the main gate, Beverly Rhodes stepped out of the office. In her eyes I detected a mixture of curiosity, awe, and envy. I smiled and . . .

"Hey, snap to, young lady," Pat said. "I got another job for you." He led me down the aisle to a framelike device that was mounted on a four-foot metal post. "Now, this here jig holds a nose cone while you work on it. Let me show you."

I watched as he mounted a three-foot metal semicircle on the jig and drilled a series of holes in it, first on one side, then on the other. Next, he picked up two six-inch ribs which contained holes that matched those he had drilled. Using screws, he attached both ribs to the cone.

"That's it," he said. "Now you do one."

It took me a lot longer than Pat to do the job, but when I finished, he said it looked good. "Just one thing," he said. "Once in a while, you'll have a rib that doesn't lie flat against the cone after you've installed it. When that happens, just take this hammer here and tap it until it fits snug. Got it?"

I nodded, anxious to get to work. To think that I, Marjorie Ellison, was actually going to be working on a bomber, and that in a few weeks that bomber might be used to strike a mortal blow at the enemy!

By the time the afternoon break came, I was putting out a nose cone every ten minutes. But then it happened—I found a rib that wouldn't lie flat. Well, I know how to take care of *that*, I thought, reaching for the hammer. But someone must have taken it. Well,

I thought, a hammer's a hammer, so I got one from the next workbench.

After a dozen light taps, the job was done. I put the cone on top of the pile of completed work and reached for the next one, and the next, and the next, congratulating myself on my speed and efficiency.

"And now for the award for the employee of the year, Marjorie Ellison."

Blushing modestly, I rose from my seat in the audience and walked toward the stage. After accepting my plaque, I faced my fellow workers. "I wish to share the honor of this award with my parents, who have always encouraged me to do my best, and to my leadman, who . . ."

"Hey, young lady, how did this happen?" asked Pat.

I looked up from my work to see that he was holding a nose cone. "How did what happen?"

"This just came back from inspection. See, it's all scratched and scarred—perfect places for rust to attack it."

"But the rib wouldn't lie flat. I just . . ."

"Ah, but you used the wrong hammer, one with a metal head, not the one I left with you."

"Someone took that one, and I wanted to get the job done fast, and . . ."

"The right tool for the job—that's the rule around here," Pat said. "We've got men out there who are depending on these planes to get them back to their bases safe and sound. Can't have anyone here cutting corners."

I nodded, hoping the tears wouldn't spill out right there in front of everyone. "I won't do it again. I promise."

My first day, I thought as Pat walked away. My very first day and I ruin a nose cone. What if that inspector hadn't seen the damage? I gritted my teeth, hearing the whine of a failed airplane engine, picturing it plunging into the ocean with its crew aboard. Had Dad been right? Had Miss Hatchet-face been right? Would our country's fighting men have been better off if I had stayed home this summer?

Chapter 21

*N*O MORE MISTAKES. THAT'S WHAT I PROMISED MYSELF EVERY
morning as I picked up my drill. And each afternoon as Larry and
I walked home, I concealed a quiet pride that no more of my nose
cones had been rejected by the inspectors. Since I'd never told
Larry about my mistake, I wouldn't have felt justified in telling
him about my success.

I hadn't told Dad about my mistake either, but that didn't stop
me from telling him about the compliment that Pat paid me one
day in late August. "My leadman says I'm one of his best workers,"
I announced that night, just before the news came on.

Dad nodded. "I wouldn't have expected any less from you." Not
what could be described as an enthusiastic response, but I knew
it was his way of saying I'd measured up to his high standards.
His words took the edge off the sharp disappointment I'd felt to
find—for the seventh day in a row—there'd been no letter from
Prentice.

"What a nice thing to say," Mom said. "And from what I've
heard about Pat, I doubt he hands out praise like penny candy."
She reached across the table and squeezed my hand.

Penny candy. My sense of accomplishment was diluted by a
feeling of desolation and of loss. All those licorice ropes and hore-

hound drops I'd bought from the Narasakis. All the warmth and acceptance I'd found in their little store. The memories were there, stronger than ever, but Mr. Narasaki was gone forever, and just last week Kaye had written and told me about the telegram her mother had received. "Killed in action," it had said. So Paul, too, was gone—Paul with his friendly, conspiratorial winks and his dream of becoming a doctor so he could ease the suffering of his fellow human beings. "We regret to inform you," the government had said, but regret is a cold, inadequate word when it's measured against the grief that the Narasakis must be feeling.

"How about some more of those spuds?" Dad asked. "A man could starve around here before anyone offers him anything." He flicked on the radio.

Mom grabbed the bowl of potatoes and held them out of his reach. "John, where are your manners? Say please, or you won't get another bite."

"Oh, for gosh sakes. All right. *Please.*" Dad's lips twitched as a shadow of a smile passed over them.

Mom's eyes contained a mischievous glint when she turned to look at me. She'd just had another small success, one of many she'd had since she had started to work. Evidently having her own paycheck, knowing that she was valuable to someone outside of her family, had given her the courage to stand up to Dad's petty tyrannies and his rudeness. Slowly, day by day, I'd seen the sparkle develop in her personality, seen her change from a meek housewife to a spunky human being, one whom Dad was still trying to understand, but one with whom he appeared to be intrigued.

"Lucky Strike Green has gone to war," the announcer said. I was wondering how that was going to help defeat the Axis, when Gabriel Heatter came on the air. "Ah, yes, there's good news tonight," he said. "Troops from the First Marine Division have made a successful landing on the beach at Guadalcanal in the Solomon Islands. Initial reports say there were few casualties, and . . ."

"The First Marines," Mom gasped. "That's Dave's division! Just a few casualties. What does that mean? Fifty, a hundred? What if he is one of them?" She put her hands over her face. "I can't stand it anymore . . . this waiting, this not knowing."

Dad got up, walked around the table, and bent over her. "Dorothy . . . don't . . . it'll be all right. They wouldn't send the whole division to invade one little island. Chances are Dave wasn't even there." His words were meant to reassure us, but one look at his stricken face told me he was as distraught as Mom was. The evening news, which at one time had seemed to set Dad apart from us, now bound us together in our anxious concern for my brother.

Finding it too painful to witness my parents' distress, I riveted my attention on the empty chair across the table from me. How many times had Dave kicked my ankles so he could see me jump? If I could only feel those size elevens right now, my smile would tell him I now know what I should have known all along—that the clumsy physical contact was his way of demonstrating his affection. Panic gripped me . . . a series of images and sounds flickered on and off in my memory . . . Dave's sudden chuckle when he'd read a comical passage in a book . . . the sound of his penny loafers—clunk, clunk—as he threw them into a corner of his room . . . his exasperating, inevitable "hey, kid." I squeezed my eyes shut to hold back the tears.

When the news was over, Dad turned the radio off. For a few minutes, the only sounds were the scraping of forks on plates and the clinks of cups being placed on saucers. It was Dad who spoke first. "We can be grateful for one thing. The Japs are finally on the run." He stood up, studied his map for a minute, then stuck a white pin in it.

"I want to win this war as much as anyone." Mom's voice broke. "But if I have to lose my son doing it, will it be worthwhile?" A tear crept down her cheek and she wiped it away with her napkin.

"Don't . . . don't." I reached out to touch her but then pulled my hand back when Dad came between us. Forgotten, ignored, I stood outside the little circle of my parents' world, but there was no resentment in my heart. My own anguish was soothed by observing the gentleness of my father's expression, the soft touch of his hands on my mother's shoulders, the way she leaned toward him, placing her head on his chest, drawing comfort from him. Perhaps for the first time in my life, I saw my mother and father as human beings who could be hurt and defenseless—two people who turned to each other for strength when their individual burdens were too much to bear.

"Dorothy . . ." Dad's voice was low. "We have to be strong for Dave."

Mom lifted her head and took a deep breath. "You're right, of course." She started collecting the dishes. "Keep busy, that's the trick. Don't dwell on things. Marjorie, hand me that platter." A few minutes later, she was in the kitchen, moving from counter to sink, wiping down the stove, scraping dishes, while I stood unnoticed in the corner, marveling at her ability to immerse herself in work while I was immobilized. I walked onto the back porch and looked down at the bay. A couple of fighter planes flew overhead. When they had passed, I heard a cricket chirping, a foghorn lowing like a neglected calf. The same sounds Dave and I used to hear when we camped out in our backyard under a blanket tent and as we played school on the steps.

* * *

The days crept by with no word from Dave and nothing from Prentice either. The worry was with me all the time, even on my last day of work when everyone was saying good-bye to me.

"We'll miss you, kid," Pat said. "I'll save you a spot on the jig for next summer."

Arlene hugged me. "Don't forget what I said about not tyin' yerself down too soon."

I hugged her back. "And don't forget what *I* said about giving Earl a chance."

"I will," she said. "But it's mighty hard to keep lovin' someone who's so far away. Sometimes it's almost as if . . . well, as if it was all nothin' but a dream . . . that it never really happened, and that it's only what's goin' on here that's real." She lowered her voice. "You know, sometimes I have a hard time rememberin' what Earl looks like unless there's a picture of him right in front of me."

"You have my number," I said. "Call me if you want someone to go out with, okay?"

As I clocked out for the last time, Arlene's words tugged at me. Maybe that old saying is true—out of sight, out of mind. I still thought of Ellen as my best friend, but it was getting harder and harder to write to her about the important things in my life. Is it really possible to put your real thoughts and feelings down on paper? Maybe she was having the same problem, because she kept telling me about the kids she was meeting and about getting a letter from Jack, but there was nothing that let me know if she felt the same persistent stirrings that I did whenever I remembered Prentice's kiss, or if she had ever dreamed of Jack's arms encircling her, pressing her to him. Or how her father's death had affected her—I mean *really* affected her. Not all that stuff about missing him—I knew that already—but how did she feel about his being down there at the bottom of the bay? Did she agonize over what he must have felt and thought as his ship floundered and sank?

And what was it that Arlene had said? She was having trouble remembering what her husband looked like. I hadn't told Ellen —I hadn't admitted it even to myself—but lately when I thought about Prentice, his image was like an out-of-focus snapshot. Oh, I could picture the way his eyes crinkle up when he laughs and that little gap between his front teeth and the way he compresses his lips when he's concentrating on something important. But when it came to putting all the pieces together to make a complete face, I couldn't, and the harder I tried, the more disconnected the image became.

Does that mean I'm falling out of love with him? The sudden idea unsettled me. No, no. It can't mean that. There's a song that says that distance and time won't tear us apart. I believe—I believe—I *know* that when the war's over . . .

There it was—the troop ship that had carried Prentice back to my waiting arms. I strained my eyes, trying to pick him out of all the hundreds of men that were filing down the gangplank, trying to hear his voice over all the other voices. And then I saw him! Older, thinner, his face drawn from exhaustion, but definitely Prentice. He strode toward me, his arms outstretched. My heart pounded as . . .

"Hey, snap out of it." Larry waved his hand in front of my face.

I wondered how long he'd been standing there waiting for me to notice him. "Sorry. I was thinking about something." We walked toward Pacific Coast Highway.

"So, how was your last day of work?"

"Great. I'm going to miss it."

"But I bet you'll like getting back in school. Oh, did I tell you my transfer came through? I'll be working swing shift so I can take a couple of classes at State."

"Boy, that'll keep you busy. Not much time for any social life."

"Don't have much of that anyway."

I gave him a sideways look. "Doesn't have to be that way. Beverly likes you."

Larry laughed. "As a matter of fact, I've taken her out a couple of times. She's a lot of fun."

No doubt, I thought. As we continued our walk home, I veered away from the subject of Beverly Rhodes, wondering why I'd brought it up in the first place, puzzled as to why it made me so uncomfortable.

We turned onto Guy Street and I saw an old green car parked in front of our house. A warning buzzer sounded in my head when I saw the gray-haired, stoop-shouldered man in a Western Union uniform ringing our doorbell.

The man walked toward me. He was carrying a yellow envelope. I put up my hand, trying to ward off the blow I knew was coming.

Chapter 22

DO YOU LIVE HERE?" THE MAN ASKED IN A QUAVERY VOICE. "This is for John Ellison."

I must have nodded yes, because he handed me a pen and a clipboard. "Sign here, please." I searched his face for some hint of assurance, but he looked away from me. How many telegrams had he delivered to homes such as ours—homes that displayed the blue star denoting a family member in the service? How many anxious, desperate eyes had he avoided?

My fingers were so numb that I had trouble guiding the pen over the yellow, lined paper. I wished I could run into the house, pretend I'd never seen this messenger, that this was a bad dream.

"Thank you, miss. God be with you." The man touched the rim of his visored cap, shuffled to his car, and drove away.

I was dimly aware that several soldiers had gathered across the street and were looking at us, their faces solemn. "Larry." I finally managed to force the sound through my throat. "Should I open it?" Please tell me not to. Don't make me look at those words.

"I think so," he replied. "It'll make it easier for your folks if you tell them."

I shoved the envelope at him, my fingers, my entire body,

rejecting it. "I can't. You do it. You read it to me." No, don't. I can't bear to hear it.

Larry pried the flap open and took the telegram out. His eyes scanned the page. "He's missing." He looked at me. "But he's not dead. Missing can mean a lot of things, not necessarily dead."

When Doris had told me about their telegram, I had said almost those same words to her, and I had believed them. But that was before today, before it was someone close to *me* who was missing.

Larry followed me into the house, placed the telegram on the table, then walked to the telephone. "Better call Mom to tell her I'll be late," he said.

"Oh, you don't have to stay." My gaze was focused on the telegram. "I'll be all right."

"Maybe so, but I'm sticking around anyway."

While he talked to his mother, I walked to the window and looked down at the bay. The water shimmered and rippled as the breeze passed over it; the golden red rays of the setting sun slanted over Point Loma; a large naval vessel was outlined on the horizon. Every detail was the same as it had always been, but each was more sharply defined than ever before.

Larry hung up the receiver and took my hand in his and I was comforted by his presence the same as I had been when I'd read about Mr. Narasaki's death. I should put on a pot of coffee, I thought. I should start to fix dinner, but how can I do those ordinary things at this extraordinary time? How do other people carry on when they're struck by tragedy? Ellen and her mother seem to be doing all right, but Doris's mother is falling to pieces. What about us? I pictured Dad flying into a blind, helpless rage, striking out at everything in his path, my mother crumpling like a rag doll with all of its stuffing removed.

And what about *me*? Would I get over feeling numb? How could

I go to school, do the meaningless things that make up my day, with this shadow hanging over me?

"Do you want me to break the news?"

I'd almost forgotten that Larry was here. "No, I'll do it." But how? Should I lead up to it, prolonging the torture? Or should I just blurt it out? Maybe Larry *should* do it—maybe—but it was too late to change my mind—I heard Mom's and Dad's footsteps on the front porch—grab the telegram—stick it under my purse—can't let them see it—not until I tell them . . .

"Larry! How good to see you." Mom's voice was bright with happy surprise. She took off her coat, placed her purse beside mine, her hand inches away from the telegram.

"Well, for gosh sake, sit down and take a load off your feet," said Dad, motioning toward a chair.

I put my hand up, signaling him to be quiet. "Wait. I have something to tell you. When we got home today, there was a . . . there was a . . ." Suddenly, all the tears I'd been holding back gushed out. It was Larry who pulled the telegram from under my purse, Larry who said the words that I'd been unable to say. I could only watch helplessly as Dad swayed, his face turning gray as his knees seem to buckle and he sat down heavily on the couch; as Mom rushed to him, sat beside him, put her trembling hand on his arm, her eyes widening as she read the telegram that Larry handed to her.

I sat on the edge of a dining-room chair, hating myself for being so weak, so ineffectual, feeling an unreasonable resentment toward Larry for doing the job that I should have done. How ironic that I—who wanted to be a writer—had been unable to find the words to ease my parents' shock or to comfort them.

"He's only missing," I said. "Like Doris's dad. Missing can be a lot of things. Some of those guys show up." Please, Dad, tell me they do, I begged silently. If you say so, maybe I'll believe it. But Dad just sat there, his hand on the top of Mom's, saying nothing. Larry moved toward the door, opened the screen, nodding to me. "See you tomorrow," he said. "Call me if I can help." I nodded back, too numb to reply.

I was beginning to wonder if my folks would ever move again when Mom got up and went into the kitchen. "We have to eat. I'll throw something together. Marjorie, would you please set the . . . set the . . ." She stopped, threw her arms around me, and sobbed quietly. My tears mingled with hers. "I love you, Mom," I said.

"I love you, too." She took her apron off its hook and wiped her face with it. "You may be all we have left, you know. If Dave . . ." She tied the apron around her waist and reached for a pot. "Enough of this. He's going to be fine and we're going to go on about our business. Creamed tuna on toast, that's what we'll have. It's quick and nourishing. Open up a can of peas."

A few minutes later it hit me—Dave's missing in action and what are we doing? Fixing tuna on toast! From somewhere deep inside of her, Mom had dredged up the strength to do these small tasks, but I couldn't—I just couldn't face eating and talking to people as if nothing's happened when I should be doing something to help find Dave—to bring him home—to . . .

Day after day, I continued my fruitless search. Fruitless, that is, until I showed his picture to an army sergeant who'd just walked off a troop ship.

"I think this guy was on that last island we captured," he said. "In fact, I'm sure of it. Some of my men got lost in the jungle, and it was he who led them to safety. Before I got a chance to thank him, he disappeared."

There it was—my first clue. He was in that jungle—the jungle with all of those wild beasts and disease-bearing insects—and it was up to me to find him—up to me to . . .

How stupid. There's no way I can help get Dave back, so here I am fixing white sauce. I picked up a spoon and traced a path through the thickening liquid. The bubbles on its surface formed, then popped, then formed again and popped again. Just like my dreams. What's the use of wanting to do great, heroic things? Even before I finish thinking about them, *pop!* they're gone forever.

"Do you want to call Doris, or should I?" Mom's voice seemed to come from far away.

Doris! I hadn't even thought of her. "Would you? . . . No, I'll do it." I turned off the fire and put a lid on the pan. "Might as well get it over with."

Her dad's missing, I thought as I dialed the telephone. Her mom drinks too much. And now this. "Doris? I—I don't know exactly how to tell you, but . . . well, we just found out that—it's Dave—he's missing."

There was a gasp on the other end of the line. "No, not him, too." Doris's voice was a hoarse whisper.

"You all right?" I asked, knowing that was the dumbest thing I could say.

"All right?" Doris's laugh startled me. "All right? Sure, I'm just fine." She was quiet for a few seconds. When she spoke again, her voice was harsh. "Those dirty Japs. I hate them. I hate all of them."

"I don't blame you. I don't blame you one little bit." I started to cry again. "I'll talk to you later, okay?" As I put the receiver back on the hook, Dad walked over to me and stroked my hair. "He'll be all right, honey."

The tenderness in his voice broke through the barrier that had built up between us, and I put my arms around his waist. "Will he, Daddy? Do you promise?"

"Of course I promise. Now, be a good little girl and help get dinner on the table." Dad put his arms on my shoulders. "And stop that crying. I tell you, Dave's going to get through this war just fine."

I nodded, for a moment overcome by a sudden surge of love for my father, wishing I could sit in his lap, retreat from the troubles of the world as I did when I was small.

"Marjorie, dinner's almost ready. Is the table set yet?" Mom's brisk voice propelled me into action. The normalcy of smoothing down the cloth, placing the plates and napkins and silverware, took the edge off the anguish the telegram had caused. This little everyday task would get me through the next few minutes; other chores would get me through the evening and the next day and the next. I looked at my father, heard my mother rustling about in the kitchen, and knew that I could draw upon their strength until I developed enough of my own.

Chapter 23

*S*LEEP WAS A LONG TIME COMING THAT NIGHT AND WHEN IT did, I dreamed that Dave and I had put up a lemonade stand at the top of the hill. Cars drove past, and pedestrians strolled by, but no one seemed to take notice of us until an army truck stopped and several soldiers got out. Dave and I smiled at each other and reached for the pitcher, eager to serve our first customers. But then I looked up and saw that the soldiers weren't Americans—they were Japanese. Dave grabbed my hand and pulled me along after him. We ran for our lives, but right behind us were the heavy sounds of booted feet running—drawing closer—closer . . .

When I woke up, my heart was pounding and I was having trouble breathing. The rays of the early morning sun were slanting into my room and as my head cleared, I wondered what sort of dreams Doris had had. Frightened dreams? Angry dreams? Or had she slept at all?

At breakfast Mom and Dad talked about doing the grocery shopping and other necessary tasks, but their faces were pale and their eyes red-rimmed. I cut off a small piece of egg white, ate it, cut off another piece, until finally only the yolk remained, round and untouched in the middle of my plate. Sticking one tine of my fork into the middle of it, I watched the yellow liquid ooze out, sopped it up with my toast, concentrating on this small ceremony so I wouldn't have to think about anything else. Then the telephone rang, jarred the calm of the moment. As I picked up the receiver, Mom and Dad looked at me, their expressions expectant, yet withdrawn, hopeful, yet fearful of news of Dave.

"Marjorie? It's me," Doris said. "What are you going to do today?"

"Nothing special," I said. "Probably just stay home."

"Why don't you come to the hospital with me?"

"Oh, Doris, I can't. You know how I feel about . . ."

"Just this once," Doris said. "See what it's like. If you can't take it, I won't ask you again."

My mind flashed back to when I was a little girl and Dad was in the hospital after being burned in an accident at work. Mom had taken Dave and me to see him, but to me it was like visiting a stranger, a pale, bandaged stranger whose voice was a hoarse whisper. When Mom told me to kiss that stranger good-bye, I had buried my face in her lap, my ears filled with the moaning of the man in the neighboring bed.

"Dave's always telling me he thinks it's great that I'm volunteering," Doris said. "He'd be really proud of you if you tried it."

Present tense. She was using the present tense, even though Dave was missing. Would you really be proud of me?

"Okay, but just today, all right?" The thought of going to a hospital was distasteful, but no worse than the prospect of sitting around the house all day with nothing to do but worry about Dave and Prentice. Besides, if Doris could put aside her concerns to help others, shouldn't I at least be willing to try?

At 1:30 when Doris and I met at the streetcar landing in front of the naval hospital, I was expecting some reaction to the fact that Dave was missing. But she showed no anger, sought no comfort or reassurance, never even mentioned it. If there was pain reflected in her eyes, it was hidden behind her glasses. Her attention seemed to be focused directly on the job at hand. "These guys are just like other guys," she said as she pulled open the door leading into the foyer. "Ask them where they're from, who's their favorite bandleader, what sort of movies they like. Things you'd ask someone you met at the skating rink."

"But what if . . . ?"

Doris headed for the hallway. "No more what ifs. I can't tell you all the things that might happen. All I can do is tell you what's happened to *me*."

She led me down the hall with its smooth, shiny tile floors and its disinfectant smell, past door after door, some open, some closed. I looked straight ahead when we went by the open doors, not wanting to see any ashen faces, any bandages, any splinted arms and legs—or worse, someone who was missing an arm or a leg.

Three nurses strolled toward us, their white uniforms making soft rustly sounds. Two of them laughed at something the third one had said. An orderly came around the corner, pushing a cart loaded with cleaning supplies and tapping out the rhythm of a silent tune with the fingers of one hand. Leaning against a wall, a doctor with a stethoscope hanging around his neck was reading the Sunday comics.

My stomach tightened. How could all of these people act so natural, as if they were working in an insurance office, or a factory, instead of here, where there were men in pain, men who were maimed, men who might be—might be dying right at this moment . . . I had to fight to take a deep breath . . . I wanted to turn and run away from this place . . . to go on pretending that war was like it was in the movies, all clean with no blood, no limbs blown off, with John Wayne or Gary Cooper coming back home in one piece, while the background music rises to a crescendo and the American flag ripples triumphantly in the wind and the audience applauds. There must be heroes here, all right, but there's no music, no applause, no assurance of a happy ending.

We turned a corner and I almost bumped into a man in pajamas and a bathrobe. He was on crutches and, like a magnet, my eyes were drawn to his right leg—or what *should* have been his right leg—my gosh, it isn't there—don't stare—but I can't help staring—I have to get out of here—I can't . . .

"Sorry," I mumbled, stepping to one side, starting to turn toward the front door.

"Wait." Doris put her hand on my arm. "You've got to meet this guy. Ben, this is Marjorie. She's a brand-new volunteer."

Ben smiled, and I focused my attention on his teeth, which were white and solid and normal-looking in contrast to the lower part of his body. "Well, hi, Marjorie," he said, balancing himself on his crutches and holding out his hand. "It'll be great having another pretty face in the rec room." I made no move to take his hand, so he put it back on the rung of his crutch and leaned forward conspiratorially. "Not that we don't appreciate the nurses, but let's face it, a lot of them are over the hill."

The sound of my laugh caught me off guard, and I found myself looking directly into his eyes—youthful-looking eyes with just a hint of the pain he must be enduring. A hero, I thought. I've met a hero, but he's not tall and broad-shouldered and unscathed. He has freckles and he's thin and ordinary-looking, a lot like half the boys at San Diego High.

Doris took my arm. "See you later, Ben. We're running a little late. Come on down to the rec hall if you can."

"Sure will. Glad to have met you, Marjorie." With a strong, fluid motion, Ben planted his crutches, swung his leg forward, and continued his journey down the hall.

"It's okay," Doris said when he was out of earshot. "You'll get used to it. The trick is to think about all the things that are right with them, not the one or two things that are wrong."

Her words went right past me, because I was trying to think how Ben must have looked when he had two strong legs, the way he must have looked when he went overseas, the way Dave had looked the last time I saw him. The way Prentice had looked.

When Doris opened the swinging door of the recreation hall, I gritted my teeth, dreading the next two hours. But when I looked around, I couldn't find anything fearful or even distressing. There was just a bunch of men and boys, some in bathrobes, some in fatigues, most of them talking or reading. One boy with his arm in a sling was turning the dial on an old console radio. Soon the room was still with the soft strains of "Chattanooga Choo Choo."

Several men were involved in a card game at a big table in the center of the room. One of them looked up when we walked toward them. "Well, I was beginning to think you weren't going to show up. Wait'll I finish this round, then I'll give you a chance to get back at me for beating you at Monopoly last week."

"And I'll do it, too, Ernie. Hey, meet Marjorie. Be nice to her and maybe she'll come back once in a while."

Ernie's face was pockmarked, but he had a nice smile. "Mighty glad you're here," he said. "Doris needs all the help she can get with these wolves. Now, me, I'm different, of course."

Doris laughed. "You're different all right. You're worse than the rest of them." She moved to one side to let a man with dark glasses feel his way past her. "Hi, how are you today?" she said.

The man didn't answer, just kept making his way across the room to a sagging couch that looked as if it were being held up by the wall.

"Blind," Doris murmured. "He's in a bad way. One of the Gray Ladies told me he thinks his wife and baby would be better off without him."

The radio was playing "You'd Be So Nice to Come Home To," and in the wistful expression of a slender young man standing nearby I could read his longing for the warmth of a fireside and the feel of welcoming arms encircling his waist. My eyes suddenly felt moist, and I wanted to tell him—this stranger—that I understood and that I prayed that soon his dreams would come true. But the song ended and the moment was past.

"His name is Bob," Doris said.

"Huh?"

"That blind sailor. His name is Bob . . . go talk to him."

"Oh, no, I can't . . . what could I say?"

"Whatever you say to anyone you've just met." She pushed me toward him. "Go on. He needs some cheering up."

Woodenly, I walked across the room, hesitated before sitting on the end of the couch, relaxed a little when Bob moved as far as he could toward the other end. I don't have to do this, I thought. It's obvious he wants to be alone. I started to get up, caught Doris's glance, then took a deep breath and said, "Hi, my name's Marjorie."

There was no reply. Bob stared straight ahead, taking refuge behind his glasses.

"This is my first day here. I'm sort of nervous."

Still no answer.

"How long have you been here?"

"Coupla' months," he muttered.

"Where are you from?"

"Doesn't make no difference. I'm never goin' back." Bob stood up, then, tapping his cane back and forth in front of him, walked out the door.

My first try at cheering up a patient and I'd upset him so much he'd left the room. Oh, Dave, I know you wanted me to do this, but I don't belong here. The only time I'm brave is in my daydreams—I'm not anything like Doris, who's able to forget her troubles—who can take charge of her emotions and . . .

A man with bandages wrapped around the top of his head took Bob's place on the couch, and this time it was me who stared straight ahead, concentrating on the big picture of President Roosevelt that was hanging on the opposite wall. It was slightly askew—I should straighten it—get up and straighten it—but everyone would look at me—except the ones who have no sight . . .

"So you're the new volunteer I've been hearing about," the man said. "I'm Stan."

I glanced at him, forced myself to smile, then turned my attention back to the picture. "But I'm not a volunteer . . . just a visitor . . . just for today."

Stan nodded his head. "I understand. I saw you talking to Bob. He's got big problems, being blind and all. You tried to help him, but right now no one can do anything for him because he's not ready to be helped. The rest of us, though, are right pleased to have you here."

It was impossible to ignore the warmth in Stan's voice. When I looked at him again, my smile came easily. "Thanks. I have to admit I was feeling guilty. I'm never able to do things just right, and I always feel so bad when I make a mistake."

"Hey, you're only human, and you're just a kid . . . what are you anyway—a sophomore in high school?"

"No, a junior."

"Makes you about sixteen. I'm twenty-three, but since I got shot up, I feel near a hundred. But maybe getting wounded was a good thing, after all."

"What do you mean?"

"Now I have a chance of getting out of the service. I can be like those 4F's—run around with some GI's girl—make good money in a war plant."

"I bet most 4F's would trade places with you in a minute." Larry would, I thought.

"Naw, most of those guys are cowards, hiding behind their mother's skirts."

Just who is the coward? I was tempted to ask. Certainly not Larry, who's been humiliated and scorned again and again, but who's kept his mouth shut and kept on doing whatever he could to get this war over. Maybe *you're* the coward. Hoping your wounds will be serious enough to get you out of more combat duty. How dare you criticize Larry. You can't feel his pain. You can't . . .

What am I doing? Sitting here with a war hero and feeling nothing but anger and resentment, not even trying to understand him or like him—have to change the subject, find something else to talk about. "Hey, listen to the radio—isn't that Woody Herman?"

"Yeah, he plays a great clarinet, but I'm a Tommy Dorsey fan myself. I play the trombone a little."

Ah, a neutral subject—I grasped it, trying to ignore the conflicting emotions that still swirled around me. "My brother likes him, too. For my fifteenth birthday he took me to see him at Pacific Square." Dave, did I ever tell you what a great time I had that night . . . how Ellen envied me for having such a terrific brother?

"Some present," Stan got a faraway look in his eyes. "I keep thinking how it would be if we could get a little band together here at the hospital. One of the guys on my ward plays the piano and a marine down the hall is good on the trumpet—or so he says. And there's this nurse who has a really good voice—she's always going around singing."

"What's stopping you?"

"No instruments."

"But you could get some. I bet if I put an ad in our school paper people would donate everything you need."

Stan's face brightened. "You really think so?"

"I not only think—I *know*."

An hour later Stan and I and a couple of other guys were so busy making plans for Stan's Swing Band that I didn't notice Doris standing there waiting for me. "I hate to break this up," she said, "but it's getting late."

"Sorry, guys." I stood up and reached for my purse. "See you next week. In the meantime, see how many more band members you can find."

"Right, boss." Stan saluted me.

"Looks like you got over your jitters," Doris said as we walked down the hall toward the hospital's entrance.

"I sure did," I said, glancing into the ward we were passing. I pictured myself walking between those rows of beds . . . comforting the wounded . . . easing their misery . . .

"Miss . . . miss." The boy's voice was weak and his face was pale. I rushed to his side.

"I'm here," I said, placing my smooth hand on his feverish brow.

"Please stay with me awhile. I'm so frightened."

"I'll be here as long as you need me."

"You're an angel, a real live angel," the boy murmured as he drifted off into a restless sleep.

As the hospital door closed behind us, the image of myself as Florence Nightingale faded. The air outside smelled like cut grass, not Lysol and ether; the people out here were well and whole, unlike the remnants of war in those hospital beds; here there was the joyous sparkle of life, not the shadow of death. Why had I promised Stan I'd be back? Stan, who'd made those remarks about 4F's—who for a moment had reminded me of that man on the bus who had called Larry a slacker. How many such insults and taunts had Larry fended off? How does he feel now that Dave's missing, and he's still here, safe, protected from the enemy's bullets by a heart defect.

I was suddenly tired—too tired to think about it rationally, so I mentally packaged it up and tucked it away, telling myself that I'd examine it later, when the vivid impressions of this afternoon had become blurred, when I'd forgotten I'd ever met a one-legged man named Ben or a blind sailor named Bob.

Chapter 24

As she had promised, Doris didn't put any pressure on me to return to the naval hospital, but I couldn't ignore the offer I'd made to help with the formation of Stan's band. Not that I knew anything about music, but, as Stan said, I was the guiding spirit behind the project. Me, a guiding spirit? I'd never pictured myself in that role, but if Stan wanted to place me in such an elevated position, who was I to refuse him? Besides, if it hadn't been for an occasional movie with Doris, my weekends would have been empty without my volunteer work. As I walked past the wards, I kept my eyes focused straight ahead, thinking only about playing checkers, talking, throwing darts, and even dancing a little with the patients who were up to that much activity.

The days crept by with no word from Dave or about him, and I learned to live with the uncertainty. I suppose during that trying period, with my mother as my model, I even learned a little about being patient and forebearing. Nevertheless, there were still many times when I wept into my pillow before I fell into a restless sleep in which my dreams brought visions of Prentice and Kaye and Ellen and Dave all blending into each other, then drifting apart. When I awoke from those dreams, I felt empty and depressed, but there was no one with whom I could share my sense of abandonment. How could I expect Ellen to understand what it was like to live in a state of uncertainty? Wouldn't she just write back and say that it was better than *knowing* that the worst had happened, that at least I still had hope.

And Kaye. How could I expect her to share my problems when she'd suffered such great losses herself?

Talking to Doris was like trying to communicate with a sponge. She kept her own feelings locked up tight inside herself and simply absorbed whatever I said with little or no reaction.

Larry would have understood my sense of isolation, my resentment at being able to do nothing but wait—wait for Prentice's letters, which came infrequently—wait for some news of Dave—wait for next summer when I could return to Consolidated and help win the war. Wait for romance to come back into my life.

Yes, Larry would have understood, but since I had returned to school, I seldom saw him. Oh, occasionally he'd walk past our house and we'd say hi to each other, but he always seemed to be in a hurry, never stayed to talk over milk and cookies. Of course, I knew how busy he was, working the swing shift and going to college in the morning, but I knew that part of his distancing himself from us was because he was a 4F and Dave was a missing serviceman.

"I'd give anything if Larry and I could be friends like we used to be," I said to Doris one Saturday in early November when we were at the zoo. It was a cool, clear day and the leaves of the eucalyptus trees rustled in the brisk breeze as we watched the Himalayan bears hold their toes and rock back and forth on their rear ends. "When he—" I stopped, too shocked to continue. There was Arlene standing in front of the polar bear enclosure, holding hands with a sailor, looking up at him, laughing, just as if she'd never exchanged marriage vows with a soldier.

"What's wrong?" Doris cocked her head and looked at me.

"Nothing. It's just someone I met at Consolidated, or maybe it isn't. Hard to tell from this far away." But it was Arlene. I was sure of it. I turned away so she wouldn't see me and be embarrassed. But would she be embarrassed? Probably not. After all, she'd come right out and told me how much she missed the excitement of going out on a date. Loneliness, a lack of excitement—what flimsy excuses to break a marriage vow, I thought.

Doris and I moved on to the seal enclosures, where a huge grandfatherly looking walrus was sunning himself while two smaller ones floated in the pool. During my past trips to the zoo, I had always been entranced by the behavior of the various animals, but right now I was distracted by what I had just seen. "What if Dave is gone for a long time—like for a year or two?" I asked Doris. "Are you going to wait for him, or will you start going out with other boys?"

An Alaskan fur seal honked and slid into the water while I waited for Doris's answer. "I've never met anyone as nice as Dave." Her voice was thoughtful. "The first time he asked me to go out, I couldn't believe my luck. I mean look at me—I'm sure no Veronica Lake."

"But what if—?"

"But what if Dave keeps on being missing, and what if someone *does* ask me for a date? The way I feel most of the time I'd say no, but sometimes I get really lonely and Mom gets to be more of a problem than usual and I'd give anything to walk along the beach holding a boy's hand. Just for an hour, just to get over feeling sad." She gave me a questioning look. "Why are you asking me all this stuff?"

"Oh, no reason." But there *is* a reason, I thought. What Arlene is doing isn't right because she's married. But what if she wasn't married—only going steady or just engaged? Would that make a difference? Would it be all right to go skating with Donnie if it kept me from going crazy from loneliness? Because I will go crazy if I have to go through this whole war waiting for my life to begin, waiting to have someone tell me I'm pretty or a good skater, or . . . well, to hold my hand or even kiss me.

Prentice. There he is facing bullets and I'm actually thinking about letting someone else kiss me. Who am I to judge Arlene anyway? But maybe if I throw myself into my work at the hospital, learn to deal gracefully with the harsh realities that exist there, pattern myself after someone like Mrs. Miniver—secure in my love, facing an uncertain future with courage and chin held high —maybe I'll be able to resist the temptations that seem to be growing stronger every day.

If there were only some way I could stop those dreams—the ones in which a handsome uniformed stranger is holding me in his arms, sweeping me away to a magical land where nothing matters except our love . . . where . . .

"Hey, let's go watch the monkeys," Doris said, tugging at the sleeve of my jacket.

"Sure." I followed her, wishing with all my heart that Prentice had come right out and asked me to wait for him, that he had given me one of his marine insignia to wear on my sweater so everyone would know I had a sweetheart in the service. The fact that I had no tangible symbol of our romance sometimes made it hard to keep alive the memories of our brief time together. Deep inside me, a faint voice had started whispering a thought that I stubbornly refused to recognize—that the bond between Prentice and me, which had once seemed so indestructible, now appeared to be fraying.

* * *

Donnie was standing on the corner when I got home that afternoon. "How ya'll doin'?" he asked. "Great to have the sun after all that rain, ain't it?"

"Sure is. My girlfriend and I went to the zoo this morning. Have you been there yet?"

He shook his head. "Waitin' till you find time to show me around."

It was hard to turn him down when he smiled like that, and I felt myself weakening. Who knows what would have happened if the mailman hadn't come up the hill at that exact moment? He was sorting out a handful of letters and when he came to one envelope, he pulled it out and waved it at me. "V-mail," he said. "Always glad to deliver those."

The small envelope he gave me was so smudged and wrinkled I couldn't make out the postmark at all, but I did recognize the cramped handwriting that spelled out "The Ellisons, 1811 Guy St. San Diego, Calif." It was *Dave's* handwriting—at that moment the most beautiful handwriting in the world. As I looked at the return address to make sure my imagination wasn't playing tricks on me, the slow pounding in my heart echoed in my ears.

But it wasn't my imagination! There it was—Pfc. David C. Ellison, FPO, San Francisco, Calif. "It's from Dave!" I shouted. "Donnie, Dave's all right. Oh, I've got to tell Mom!"

I caught a glimpse of Donnie's grin before I raced up the front steps and into the house. "Mom!" I shouted. "Where are you?" No answer. Across the porch, down the steps, down the driveway. There she was, taking a sheet down from the clothesline.

"It's a letter from Dave!" I ran across the lawn and shoved the envelope into her hand. "Open it. Hurry. I can't wait."

Mom dropped a clothespin on the grass as she looked at the return address. "It really is, isn't it? My prayers have been answered." Fingers trembling, she opened the letter and started reading out loud. "September 20, somewhere in the Pacific."

September 20. The telegram had been dated September 28. Mom . . . stop. Nothing's changed.

But she kept right on reading, apparently oblivious to the fact that we had become the victims of a cruel trick of fate.

Dearest Mom and all,

Don't have much time because we're going to be moving out any minute now. Don't know what's going to happen, but almost anything's better than . . .

Mom's voice faded out, and as the awful realization swept over her, her shoulders slumped. "Marjorie . . . the date . . . the date." She handed the letter to me.

"I know, Mom." I squinted at the bottom half of the page, trying to make out the cramped handwriting although I knew the words were meaningless.

. . . almost anything's better than sitting around waiting, policing the area, washing out socks and skivvies, playing cards.

Well, Sarge just told us to get our stuff together. I'll get someone to put this in the mail for me.

Love to all,
Dave

So, someone else had mailed that letter, and he must have forgotten to send it right away, or else the mail got mixed up.

Whatever the reason, in the space of a few seconds we had gone from indescribable joy to utter despair.

Standing there with the clothes flapping in the quickening wind off the bay, I was so full of pain and anger that I found myself unable to reach out and comfort my mother. Silently, like robots, we pulled clothespins from the line, put them in a cloth bag, piled sheets and towels, work shirts, and socks and slips into the wicker laundry basket. Then, bending over in unison, we picked up the basket and carried it between us up the back steps and into the house. As we placed it on the kitchen counter, Mom turned to me, her hazel eyes dry, her chin firm. "Don't tell your father about this. It would upset him so."

From deep in the recesses of my memory an image appeared. It was the day before my twelfth birthday and I was placing some freshly ironed napkins in the top drawer of the buffet when a tissue-wrapped object in the back of the drawer piqued my curiosity. As I peeled off the paper to reveal a bicycle horn, my mother came into the room. "Oh, no," she said. "It's your birthday present from Dave. Don't tell him you found it. He'd be so disappointed."

Was it just my mother, or did every mother make it her mission to insulate the members of her family from disappointment and pain? How many times had I seen her smooth over an argument between Dad and Dave, intervene when she realized that Dad was putting up obstacles between me and something I wanted? And now she was protecting Dad himself. Beneath my mother's meek, mild surface, she was the strong one in the family, the one whose spirit would bend, but never break.

Mom went into her bedroom and closed the door. I followed her, started to knock, but pulled back, knowing there was nothing I could do or say that would ease her pain. She needed some time alone. I, on the other hand, needed to reach out for help, to talk to someone. I dialed Doris's number. Six rings, no answer. Larry. He'll understand. I dialed again, and Mrs. Woods answered almost immediately.

"Is Larry there?" I asked.

"Yes, Marjorie, but he's in the shower. He's going out in a little while."

"Going out?"

"Yes, with a girl named Beverly. He seems quite taken with her."

Beverly! Just when I need him the most he's going out with *Beverly*. "Oh, well, it isn't important. Don't bother to tell him I called."

"Are you sure? Maybe he'll have a few minutes before he leaves."

"No, no, it's all right. Thanks anyway." I hung up, realizing I'd been gripping the receiver so tight my knuckles had turned white. For several minutes I just sat there, staring at the wall. Why did I hate to think about Larry being with Beverly? Why was I thinking about the way Larry laughed? Why did I feel a deep ache in my stomach?

I stood up and stared out the window at the silhouette of Point Loma against the horizon. Prentice. Larry. Larry. Prentice. Larry and Beverly. The images chased each other around my head in a confused tangle. And then I thought of Dave's letter and the terrible sadness crowded the images out.

Chapter 25

*R*OMMEL'S AFRIKA CORPS ON THE RUN! SOVIET OFFENSIVE OVER-
WHELMS NAZIS. JAP BATTLESHIP SUNK AT GUADALCANAL. During
October and November the daily headlines announced the heart-
ening news. To keep track of the Allied advances, Dad still moved
the pins around on his map, but he did it quietly, almost auto-
matically, with no mutterings of "Go get 'em, leathernecks," or
"That'll show you, Shickelgruber."

Mom was quiet, too. She went to work, did the ironing, dusted
the furniture, but it was as if she was a robot doing all those
things—that letter from Dave had taken all the life out of both
of my parents. As for me, when I wasn't angry, I was sad and
confused, and the worst part was that I felt more alone than I ever
had in my entire life. Mom and Dad were locked in their own
painful world. Doris had her hands full with her own problems.
And Larry—if I saw him passing by our house, he barely took the
time to say hi before he rushed on.

Occasionally, on an especially bad day, I convinced myself that
Larry's neglect was a result, not of his sensitivity about not being
in the service, but of his spending so much time with Beverly
Rhodes. At those times, I didn't care much whether I ever saw

him again or not. If his social life was more important than his old friends . . . well, who needed him?

When Thanksgiving came, Mom insisted on making the usual dinner. "Dave would want it that way," she said, and I knew that was the only reason she would go to all the trouble. To make the house seem less empty, she told me to invite Donnie and a couple of his buddies from across the street. Right at two o'clock they were at our front door. When I answered their knock, Donnie shoved a bouquet of sweet peas and poppies at me. "Grew 'em myself," he said, a grin spread across his freckled face. "Right outside my tent."

As I took the flowers, his fingers touched mine and my heart took a little jump. "Thanks, they're really pretty," I murmured, burying my nose in their soft fragrance. While our guests hung their jacket and caps on the coat rack, I went into the kitchen to get a vase and to get a grip on my jumbled emotions. It had been a long time since a boy had touched my hand. How good it felt. I thought that maybe I should say yes the next time Donnie asked me for a date. For a moment Prentice's face flashed into my mind, but then the vision grew blurry and faded away. It had been over two weeks since his last letter, but I had promised myself I wouldn't think about that.

Mom had hoped that Donnie and his friends would liven up our holiday dinner, and they more than fulfilled her expectations. While Dad carved the turkey and Mom poured the milk and coffee, our guests kept us laughing with stories about their life in the service.

"Why, since I've been in the yew-ess army, ah've been called dogface so many times, I bark when Sarge is takin' roll call," Donnie said.

"That's nuthin," said one of his buddies, a short, red-faced corporal. "Lately, when I dig a foxhole, I forgit to use a shovel."

The third soldier helped himself to another serving of candied yams. "This is the best chow I've had since I left home. By the time our supper gets to us, the soup has usually jelled and the Jell-O's turned to soup."

Even Dad had shed his cloak of aloofness by the time Mom served the pie, and Donnie winked at me as if we were sharing some friendly sort of secret. Paul Narasaki used to wink at me that way. For a moment the memory shut out the sound of Dad's chuckle, and I resented Donnie for reminding me that the Narasakis had little to be thankful for on this day.

My resentment passed as quickly as it had appeared, because I realized that Donnie had given me a sign that he understood how solemn and quiet our Thanksgiving would have been without our guests. It suddenly struck me that he was sitting in Dave's chair, the chair that had been almost a hallowed place ever since that farewell dinner last February. And I knew that Dave would have approved of Mom's decision to have a homesick serviceman there in his stead.

Just as I took my first bite of pie, there was a knock at the front door and I almost choked. It can't be Larry, I thought. When I'd asked him to drop by and have dessert with us, he'd said he would try but not to count on him. That's all right, I wanted to tell him. I stopped counting on you a long time ago.

But when Mom opened the door, I heard her say "Well, look who's here. Come on in," and Larry stepped into the front room. He glanced at me, then at Donnie, and his smile seemed to freeze. "Sorry, I can't stay," he said. "Just wanted to wish you folks a happy Thanksgiving."

"Nonsense." Mom took his arm and led him to the table. "I'll get a chair from the kitchen and cut you a piece of pie. Surely, you have enough time for that."

Larry had never had any more luck arguing with Mom than I had. A few minutes later he was seated between Donnie and one of his friends on the side of the table opposite me. The joking and talking seemed to quiet down a little as Larry took a bite of his pie, and when I looked at Donnie, I sensed a tenseness in the way he held his head and in the expression on his face. How could Mom have been so insensitive as to insist on Larry's staying? But then I remembered it had been me who had invited him in the first place—me who had put him in this awkward position. Perhaps it was me who should shout, sure he's a 4F, but he's not a coward. It takes courage to face what he has to face every day, and he's doing everything he can to help win the war, and if he could, he'd be right there in the front lines facing bombs and bullets.

But of course I couldn't say anything like that. For one thing, Donnie wouldn't believe it, and for another, Larry would never forgive me for making excuses for him.

The tension in the room was thick by the time Larry finished his pie. When he stood up to say good-bye, I was glad he was leaving, not so much for me, but for him. "See you around," I said as I walked him to the door.

"Sure," he replied, his voice low, and then he walked down the steps, his shoulders slumped, his attitude so different from his usual forward-looking, optimistic air.

"Larry," I called after him.

He turned to look at me. "What?"

"Happy Thanksgiving."

"Thanks."

* * *

The happy mood that had filled our house earlier had faded by the time Donnie said good-bye as we stood on the porch. His buddies had gone back to camp, probably with a shared understanding that Donnie would want to be alone with me. The sun had almost disappeared behind Point Loma, and the harsh song of a mockingbird perched on a telephone wire provided a counterpoint to the brisk Marine Corps band music that floated up from the drill field on the base. Donnie reached for my hand. I let him take it.

"Had a real good time today," he said.

"Thanks. We're glad you could come."

He was quiet for a moment. "Sure would like it if you'd go out with me sometime."

His hand felt good in mine. "Well, maybe we can." As I said the words, I felt a small part of my past slip away.

"Are you joshin' me? How about this weekend? I still haven't seen that famous zoo of yours."

Now was the time to tell him about Prentice, but I had no desire to make that surprised grin fade.

"Why not? Maybe Sunday afternoon. Can you get a pass?"

"Don't see no problem there. Let's get an early start."

"Okay. I'll pack a lunch."

"Great." He leaned forward and gave me a light kiss on my cheek. "See you then." Whistling, he ran down the steps and across the street as the light scent of honeysuckle wafted past me, filling me with longing for a moment that now seemed to live only in my imagination.

That night, after the dishes were done and while Mom and Dad were listening to the radio, I tried to write to Prentice. But it was hard to tell him about our Thanksgiving dinner without including the fact that we had had company. I put the pencil down and touched my face where Donnie had given me that quick kiss. From where I sat I could see the camp and the shadowy figures that were silhouetted against the lamplight in the tents. One of those figures might be Donnie. Was he looking at our house—at this window? I drew the shade and started writing again. "Dear Prentice, Thanksgiving was awful without you. Mom fixed turkey and everything, but I know that she was thinking about Dave and so was Dad. Maybe we should have just skipped the whole thing. . . ."

Somehow I finished the letter without telling a lie, but without saying anything about Donnie being there, which I suppose wasn't exactly telling the truth. As I sealed the envelope, I felt guilty, but I couldn't help wondering what it would be like to have Donnie kiss me on the lips. Would I get dizzy as I did when Prentice had kissed me? Would the world seem to turn upside down? Would I dream about it afterward?

What am I doing? Am I like Arlene? Prentice, what's happening to us? All these long months I've been true to you, kept your letters under my pillow so I could touch them if I woke during the night, thrown kisses toward the ocean so the waves could carry them to you. I've tried to create a love that would last until you come back to me, and today—not quite a year after you left, I let Donnie hold my hand and I told him I'd go to the zoo with him. I've failed you, Prentice.

Actually, I've failed at a lot of things lately. Sure, I helped the men at the hospital organize a band, but I still can't look at someone who's missing a limb or who has bandages over his eyes. I still want to quit the hospital and volunteer at a U.S.O., where I can meet servicemen who aren't on crutches or in wheelchairs or trembling and feverish from a recurrence of malaria.

And what about Kaye? What had I done for her when the kids at school were bullying her and her friends? Not a thing. How many times had I decided I was too busy to stop in and visit with her parents? Too many times. Oh, yes, I'd fixed up the store after it had been vandalized, but what good had that done Mr. Narasaki? He had already died of a broken heart, never knowing how much I cared.

Ellen and I still wrote to each other, but somehow our friendship had changed. How could it stay the same, when she had gone through so much that I'd never had to experience—surviving a bombing, losing her father. I hadn't shared those things with her, so how could I understand how she felt? And how could I really be her friend unless I did understand?

I looked around my room. There was the raggedy teddy bear I'd had since I was two. There was my small desk piled high with a jumble of books and paper. There were the faded curtains and the linoleum, its floral pattern worn off in the heavily traveled areas. There was the closet door with the pencil marks that showed how I'd grown from year to year.

And there on my dresser was the enlarged snapshot of Dave and Larry and me that Mom had taken at a picnic five years ago. My gosh, had I ever been that skinny?

I looked closely at the picture of Larry. He was laughing, probably at something I'd said. Now he hardly ever laughed, at least when he was around me.

I looked around my room again. All these things were so familiar. Why, then, did I feel so different?

Deep inside, I knew the answer. It was because I had lost something big. Something really important. Something I couldn't even begin to understand.

Chapter 26

SHOULD I OR SHOULDN'T I? I MUST HAVE ASKED MYSELF THAT question at least a dozen times before Donnie showed up at our house on Sunday morning. Then, hearing his knock at the door, I knew it was too late to change my mind. Woodenly, I put on my jacket, picked up the lunch I'd packed, and met him on the front porch.

As we rode the bus and streetcar to Balboa Park, Donnie told me a string of really good jokes, but after the third or fourth one, I could only pretend to laugh. He asked questions about my school and my family, but when I answered, I was remembering how Prentice had asked me some of those same questions. When Donnie talked about his family in Tennessee, I wanted to be interested in how his uncle Joe had taught him how to skeet shoot, but instead found myself thinking about Prentice's last letter and how disappointed I'd been when all he'd discussed was the weather. "The rain never stops," he had written. "Everything's soaked all the time, including me. My biggest dream right now is to feel warm and dry for an hour or two." Where was I in that dream? Nothing he said in any of his letters mentioned wanting to hurry back to me or missing me or that kiss under the peppertree.

To be honest, although I thought about Prentice during the

day, he hadn't appeared in any of my dreams for at least three weeks. But wasn't that his fault? Doesn't love need to be nourished or fueled? How could I keep on giving love without getting anything in return?

It was while Donnie and I were in the reptile house that he apparently tired of carrying on a one-sided conversation. "You're real quiet today," he said, his eyes riveted on a boa constrictor that was gliding effortlessly in a never-ending movement over and under and around the bare branches of a small tree. "Somethin' on your mind?"

I shook my head, trying to clear away the doubts and the shadows, feeling guilty when I saw the look of genuine concern in Donnie's expression. "Oh, no. I'm having a good time." You're nice, I wanted to say. Really nice. But I wish that Prentice were standing here beside me instead of you and I know how hurt you'd be if you knew that, so, of course, I have to keep pretending and hoping you won't ask me out again.

"Well, it's natural enough for you to be a little down in the dumps with Christmas comin' on and your brother missin' and all, but I was hoping that a little outing would take your mind away from that for a while." Donnie took my arm and we drifted down the corridor in the slow-moving current of the other spectators. "But it's not all that easy to forget about someone you love, is it?"

"That's right," I replied as we stopped to watch the Gila monsters. Although I felt a responsibility to hold up my end of the conversation, my mind began circling around the word *love* and all its different meanings. The love I had for Dave and my parents—it's always been there, unnoticed, taken for granted, like the steady beating of my heart, until this crisis brought it to the surface to strengthen and unify us. On the other hand, my love for Ellen, which had been built on a foundation of shared, pleasant experiences, now seemed to be crumbling because of unpleasant experiences that couldn't be shared.

But what about my love for the Narasakis? I hadn't been able to share the loss of their store, their home, their entire way of life. I hadn't been able to put my arms around Kaye when she had lost her father or when she had heard about her brother's death. But as she poured out her grief and her anger in her letters to me, and as I expressed my own pain and remorse, the bonds between us had become stronger.

And there was my love for Prentice, which had come swiftly, unexpectedly, like a wave crashing upon a beach. I had once thought it to be indestructible, but it was now ebbing like the tide.

It's not fair that I have to live my life waiting for a word, a sign that you love me, Prentice. It's just not fair.

As the afternoon wore on, Donnie bought me some hot roasted peanuts and we shared the sandwiches and fruit I had brought and I held his hand as we walked up the long flight of stairs that bordered the largest bird cage in the world. By four o'clock, when we decided to leave, he was telling me some humorous stories about life in the service and I was surprised by the sound of my impulsive laughter and the knowledge that I hadn't thought about Prentice or Dave for over an hour.

Later, when we were standing on the sidewalk in front of my house, I again surprised myself by asking, "Want to come to Christmas dinner?" and finding that I wanted Donnie to say yes.

A broad grin creased his face. "Sure." He hesitated. "Do you suppose we could take in a movie sometime?"

"Maybe . . . why not?"

"Great. See you later." He winked and squeezed my hand, then turned, and with a bounce to his step, strode across the street.

It was less than a week later that I heard the news from one of the soldiers stationed in the camp—while I was at school that day, Donnie and eleven others in the unit had been loaded into a truck and taken to the pier to be shipped overseas.

"I'm sorry I couldn't say good-bye," he had written in the note he'd left for me. "Hope you hear from Dave soon. I'll write as soon as I get a chance. Thanks again for showing me around the zoo. I'll be thinking of you at Christmastime."

Another good-bye. I folded the paper and put it in my purse, knowing that I'd miss having him wave to me each time I left the house, that I'd miss his ever-present grin. But will I really miss *him*? I didn't know, but his sudden departure added to my feeling of loss.

Please keep him safe, I prayed. And when he comes home, let him find a girl who can love him the way I once thought I loved Prentice.

Chapter 27

"ONLY FIFTEEN SHOPPING DAYS UNTIL CHRISTMAS." "SHOP AT Marston's for all your gift items." "Season's greetings!" The holiday messages poured out every time I turned on the radio, but instead of putting me into a festive mood, each carol, each cheerful greeting, only left me more and more depressed. I was still wavering over my feelings for Prentice and worried about Dave, and to my surprise, I missed seeing Donnie's grin whenever I passed the camp.

Because of my lack of holiday spirit, the only presents I'd bought so far were those that had to be mailed early. Ellen was to receive a fuzzy stuffed cat in place of the live pet she couldn't have because her family moved around so much. I hoped Kaye would enjoy the book of poetry I'd bought for her and would understand what I was trying to say in the poem I wrote with her in mind.

How I regret
The opportunities I've never had
   The chance to dream
      and to have that dream become reality
   The chance to throw off my bonds
      and push aside the boundaries of my world
   The chance to soothe my spirit

in the scent of the honeysuckle blossom
The chance to use the power of the written word
to move people to tears and to laughter
and to bind up the wounds of my friends

With the purchase and mailing of those two gifts, my shopping came to a halt. It was too difficult to face all those ho-ho-hoing department store Santas, to hear the tidings of good will contained in the carols that were played on every radio, to plod rain-soaked along the crowded city streets, forcing a smile every time a harried shopper poked me with a package.

Meanwhile, Mom was radiating her usual holiday cheer—coming home from work to make candies and cookies to give to the neighbors, hanging a wreath on the front door, working and re-working her Christmas list. It was only occasionally, when she paused for a moment, that I could see the emptiness in her eyes and the tight lines in her face. Then, as if someone had pushed an "on" button, she threw herself back into her feverish activity.

Early one Saturday evening, I was sitting at the dining-room table writing name tags while Mom wrapped the last of her gifts and Dad was replacing a bulb that had burned out on the tree. "What's the use of all this fuss?" I blurted out. "After all, there's sure not much to celebrate."

Mom finished tying a bow before she looked at me, her face soft, her hair hanging free, giving her a youthful look. "Don't you think Dave would want us to keep up the family traditions? Don't you think he's imagining how our tree looks and the presents and the turkey and dressing?"

"But that sweater you got for him. He won't . . ." If I finished the sentence, I knew I'd cry. Instead I reached over and touched her hand. "I'm sorry. I . . ."

Mom shook her head. "Don't say it. Just try to understand . . . this is my way of getting through this thing. If I didn't have something under the tree for Dave . . . well, it would be like giving up on him, and . . ." Her chin quivered, and Dad walked over and put his hand on her shoulder. "I'm not going to give up."

I wished I could find the words to tell her how brave I thought she was. Just like those women in the movies, like Mrs. Miniver, carrying on, holding our world together in spite of all the things that were trying to tear it apart.

"There, that's that," Mom said, putting her hand on top of Dad's and smiling at me. "Would you take this stuff and put it outside."

"Sure." I took the overflowing wastepaper basket and headed for the back porch. After I dumped it into the trash can, I stood on the steps, listening to the radio in the house next door playing "Santa Claus Is Coming to Town." The two little girls who lived there were laughing and talking in high-pitched, excited voices. War or no war, they would go to bed on Christmas Eve and dream about dolls and toys, new pinafores and games, sugarplums and decorated cookies.

Our telephone rang and I hoped it wasn't anyone for me. Right now I wanted to dream a Christmas dream and wake up to find it had come true. The problem was that what I wanted couldn't be wrapped in tissue paper, then tied with a bow, and placed under a tree. I wanted to be in love with Prentice and have him in love with me. I wanted to know that Dave was still alive. I wanted Ellen and me to be the close friends that we used to be. I wanted Larry to drop in and have cookies and milk and to laugh and wink at me. I wanted my life to have some happy endings, like the ones in the movies.

In the movies, war is a glamorous, thrilling adventure, and the good guys win all the battles and come home to live happily ever after.

A stray breeze made me shiver and I picked up the wastepaper basket and walked back into the house. It was strangely quiet, the sort of quiet that's in the air just before a thunderstorm. No radio, no rustling of Dad's newspaper, no talking. I went into the dining room and felt as though a giant fist had punched me in my stomach. That look on Mom's face, and on Dad's, too—wasn't it the same look they'd had when I told them Dave was missing? Almost, but not quite. That telephone call! "Wh-what's wrong? It's not—no —it's not—" I couldn't say the words.

Mom got up and took my hand. "It's Dave. He's on his way home. We just got a call from the Red Cross."

What fantastic, glorious, wonderful news! But where was all the laughing and the cheering and the happy tears, the rushing to the telephone to tell everyone? What were they keeping from me?

"He's hurt, honey," Dad said. "We don't know how bad. But, of course, the important thing is that he's alive." He took a handkerchief from his pocket and wiped his eyes. "He's alive."

"I'm sure they wouldn't be moving him if it were anything really serious." Mom's voice was just a little too eager, a little too reassuring.

My mind started to spin. Dave was alive. But how badly injured was he? I pictured him stumbling with a cane or sitting in a wheelchair or trussed up in bed with no legs . . . no arms . . . no sight . . . I wouldn't be able to look at him . . . I wouldn't know how to talk to him.

"Marjorie, are you all right? Say something." Dad's voice came to me from someplace far away. I buried my face in his chest, sobbing, shaking. The waiting was over. Dave would be home for Christmas. Certainly that was enough for now.

Chapter 28

*D*AVE'S COMING HOME! DAVE'S COMING HOME! AS I TRAVELED to school, went from class to class, came home, studied for tests, the words flashed off and on in my head like a neon sign. Occasionally, like a small dark cloud blocking out the brightness of the sun, a nagging worry about the extent of his injuries cast a shadow over my jubilation; within moments, however, the general joyousness of the season and the knowledge that Dave was no longer facing enemy fire put the bounce back into my step.

Mom and Dad and I had taken a vote and come to a unanimous decision to, if necessary, put off our holiday celebration until Dave actually arrived in San Diego. Meanwhile, the pile of presents under the tree kept growing, and the cupboards were bursting with cranberry sauce and pickles and the makings of pumpkin and mince pies.

Five days after we got the letter from the Red Cross, we got one from Dave himself. He didn't say much, and his handwriting looked shaky, but the fact that he had been able to write it made Dad laugh right out loud and Mom sing "When Johnny Comes Marching Home Again" as she layered the potato casserole that evening. Mom couldn't carry a tune in a bucket—that's what Dad always said—but right then I knew he agreed with me that her voice sounded better than Kate Smith's, because it was the first time she'd sung since Dave had gone overseas.

Finally, on the day before Christmas Eve, the chaplain from the naval hospital called to tell us that Dave had arrived. I telephoned Doris, then Larry, but he was at work.

"But I'll tell him the minute he walks in the door," Mrs. Woods said. "I can't tell you how happy I am for all of you."

I had no idea what Larry would do when he heard the news. Maybe he'd called us on the phone. Maybe he'd drop by the house. There wasn't much time to wonder about it, because Dad was already outside, warming up the car. What great timing, I thought. If Dave had gotten here just one week later, we would have had to take the bus, because our car would have been up on blocks. Since rationing had started, it was hard to get enough gas to keep it running. "Glad to give old Betsy a rest," Dad had said. "Those boys at the front need gas a lot more than we do."

A half hour later Mom, Dad, and I were walking toward the door of Dave's ward. "Only two visitors at a time," a nurse said, raising a warning finger.

"You go," I said. "But don't wear him out so much that he won't be able to talk to me."

Mom hugged me. "We'll keep it short."

There were benches in the waiting room down the hall, but I was much too nervous to sit for long. For a while, I paced back and forth, thumbing through a six-month-old *Country Gentleman*, barely aware of the hospital sounds and smells. Of the hundreds of patients in the hospital, at this moment there was only one who had any claim to my attention.

I put the magazine back into the rack, stared out the window at the nearly empty parking lot, at the car turning in from Twelfth Street, its headlights blurred by a drizzling rain. Then, unable to stand quietly, I wandered back into the hall, almost bumping into a boy in civvies who had just come around the corner. "Excuse me," I mumbled, stepping to one side to let him pass.

"Marjorie."

Larry. Unexpected tears filled my eyes, and without thinking, I put my arms around him. His shirt smelled of grease and factory dust and perspiration—at that moment it was sweeter than the scent of honeysuckle—and when I put my head on his chest, I felt the beating of his heart, a steady, comforting rhythm that symbolized his strength, his dependability. Within an instant all the bitterness, real or imagined, that I'd felt toward him had dissolved.

A group of orderlies walked toward us, and, flustered, I backed away, looking past Larry, wishing that Mom and Dad would appear, regretting my impulsive action.

"How is he?" Larry asked.

I sniffled and fumbled in my jacket pocket for a hankie. "I don't know. I haven't seen him yet. There's something wrong with his shoulder . . . Mom and Dad are with him . . ." Oh, Larry, if you only knew how glad I am to see you, but now I've gone and ruined everything by hugging you and I know you like Beverly and I had no business doing that and I'm sorry . . . Even as those thoughts raced through my head, I wanted him to put his arms around me because I knew his touch would make me feel safe.

"Come on. Let's sit down." Larry took my arm and led me to a bench. After sitting beside me for a few moments, he cleared his throat. "I've been feeling rotten about—well, about not seeing you and your folks, but you know how busy I've been with work and school and . . ."

"You don't have to apologize. I understand. And, of course, there's Beverly."

"It hasn't anything to do with Beverly. Oh, we went out a few times, but mostly just to talk. Do you know her brother's a 4F, too?"

"Her brother? Oh, I remember something about his having infantile paralysis. Left him with that limp and . . ."

Larry put his hand on my arm. His eyes turned a darker shade of brown. "Be quiet. I'm going to bust open if I don't say this."

Startled at the harsh tone of his voice, I stared at him.

"I've kept my mouth shut because I know how you feel about Prentice and there he is overseas and I don't want to take advantage of a serviceman." His smile was feeble, and he seemed to be struggling to get the words out. "But I like you a lot, Marjorie." He lowered his gaze. "I shouldn't have said that."

My heart missed a couple of beats and when it started up again, it felt like a tom-tom in my chest. "I didn't know . . . I—I'm sorry."

Larry stood up and half turned away from me. "This is a lousy time to spring this on you, but I just had to get it out of my system. The thought of you and Prentice together . . . well . . ."

Prentice. What about him anyway? For the last few weeks I'd felt him slipping away until lately the only strong memory I had of him was that kiss and how it had made me feel, and sometimes I even wondered if that day had been nothing but a dream. Was my great love affair just another one of my fantasies?

Larry turned back to face me. "I'm the one who's sorry. I guess I should have spoken up a long time ago, but I wanted to give us both a chance to grow up a little. And then you met Prentice and I wasn't about to run around with a serviceman's girl, so I lost my chance."

But you haven't! I stopped short of actually saying the words, astonished at not only the intensity but also the depth of my feelings. This boy, who'd always been at the edges of my life, a somewhat blurry figure who came and went almost without notice, had suddenly moved center stage.

"Marjorie."

My mother's voice gave me the chance to focus on something solid and familiar, let me postpone for a moment the realization of my changed relationship with Larry.

"Larry, how glad I am that you could come. Both of you can go in now." Mom hugged me. "He's going to be fine. It's just a matter of time."

Dad came up behind Mom. "What a boy," he said. "Seems he was lost on patrol on Guadalcanal. Got captured by the Japs, but he escaped. Can you believe that boy? He escaped! Took a couple of bullets, but he . . ."

"John, will you stop talking and let the youngsters see Dave before he falls asleep. Honestly, you just go on and on sometimes." Mom pushed me in the direction of Dave's ward, but not before Larry raised his eyebrows in surprise. He'd never seen the new Mom in action before.

"Last bed on the right," Dad called as we walked down the hall. "Have him show you his Purple Heart."

I heard Mom shushing him as we entered the ward, and a few moments later I was standing over the last bed on the right and thinking Dad had made a mistake. This sallow-faced boy with the bulky bandage covering his arm and shoulder wasn't my brother! But then the patient opened his eyes and grinned. "Hey, kid. Hi, Larry. What's new?"

"Dave." I bent over to kiss his forehead. "You look so great."

"Sure I do. And so do you guys. Here we are again, the three of us, just like it's always been." His voice trailed off and his eyes closed again, but a trace of a smile remained.

I looked up at Larry. "Maybe just the way it will always be."

Larry looked down at me, a startled, happy question in his eyes, but I wasn't ready to answer that question yet. As we turned away from Dave's bed, he took my hand, lightly at first, as if waiting for my reaction, then tightening his grip when I didn't pull away. His touch feels so good, I thought. A soft warmth crept through me, not the thunderous wave of passion I'd experienced with Prentice. I sensed I was standing at the edge of something new and miraculous, but there was no feeling of impatience, of time pressing in on me. I could wait to take that first step; I could feel my way into this relationship, make my way slowly, savor it.

And when the time was right, I'd tell Doris and Ellen and Kaye. They'll all be happy for me because they're my friends and they'll want to share the good things in my life even though I couldn't share the bad things in theirs. And Prentice—yes, I'll tell him, too, because he already knows that what we shared wasn't meant to last.

When Larry and I left the ward, Mom and Dad were standing in the hall, arms entwined, faces beaming. How brave they've been through all this, I thought. And so have Larry and Doris. And what about me? I've never had the chance to perform any of those bold, awe-inspiring feats I keep imagining. All I've done is to plod through each ordinary day, doing what had to be done, waiting for a letter than might never come.

But I never lost faith that it *would* come, did I? And I did what I could in my own small way—collected salvage, bought war stamps, prepared myself for whatever emergency might come along, helped to put bombers in the air. Little things, all of them, but I had done them well.

"Hey," Larry said. "I still haven't finished my Christmas shopping. How about coming along with me?"

"Come along with you? Of course I will," I murmured just before our lips met and my head became filled with a shower of stars . . .

"Sure." I smiled up at him. "I thought I was done, but just remembered that there's still one more person on my list."

"Is this person someone special?" Larry asked, his eyes twinkling.

There was no need to hurry, to reach too far too fast. "Time will tell," I said, squeezing his hand.